The Girls from the Five Great Valleys

The Girls from the Five Great Valleys

a novel

By Elizabeth Savage

Introduction by Nancy Pearl

Text copyright © 1977 Elizabeth Savage
Introduction and Readers' Guide © 2014 Nancy Pearl

A Book Lust Rediscovery
Published by Amazon Publishing

www.apub.com

ISBN-13: 9781612183206
ISBN-10: 1612183204

Cover design by: David Drummond

Printed in the United States of America

Introduction

I FIRST READ THIS, the author's seventh novel, in 1978. My family and I had just moved to Tulsa from Stillwater, Oklahoma. I hadn't met many people yet and, even in September it was still enervatingly hot. My children were (at last) in school full time and the hours in the days seemed boundless with nothing to do. I was disinclined to leave the air-conditioned house, but knew I needed to or else I would go berserk. So, as I have always done during the bad times in my life, I went to the library. I browsed the fiction shelves of Tulsa's East Second Library (which is now named the Kendall-Whittier branch), looking for books that would help take me out of myself, off to a different time and place. A few years before I had read, and loved, *The Last Night at the Ritz* (which is also one of the baker's dozen Book Lust Rediscoveries) and was hoping the author, Elizabeth Savage, might have a new novel out. And there it was, beckoning me, shelved at the end of the other novels whose authors have a last name beginning with *Sa* (Salinger, Salter, Saramago …) and looking as though no one had checked it out before. Clearly, it was there as my reward for venturing out on my own.

A strong sense of place permeates all of Elizabeth Savage's writing. She was born in Massachusetts, attended college in Maine, and for many years she and her husband Thomas (also a novelist) split their time between Montana and the coast of Maine, the setting for many of her later novels. But wherever Savage's novels are set, the reader gets a strong sense of the "thereness" of the place, and how, in all its particularity, both physical and historical, the setting affects the lives of the characters. It becomes, in itself, almost a separate character. In most of the novels that I read I respond most strongly to the characters and their story—I have a sense of sharing their lives; I wonder what happened to them after the book ended; I fantasize about meeting them in real life. Many of them have, over the years of reading, become my friends. Being taken out of my own life that way is one of the great joys of reading for me. But in *The Girls from the Five Great Valleys* I found myself responding just as strongly to its setting. In fact, Savage's evocation of place in this novel meant so much to me that since I read it all those years ago—almost thirty-five years, now—I've suffered from a not-so-mild case of "Where I Come From" dysphoria. I think that I was somehow meant to have been born and raised in Montana—Bozeman, Cut Bank, Missoula, Billings, Helena, Thompson Falls—anywhere in the state, really, instead of in the (to me) utterly unexciting, unromantic, and unbeautiful urbanity of Detroit, Michigan, where I was in fact born, and where I spent the first eighteen years of my life.

The specific place that Savage conjures up for the reader in this novel is Missoula, Montana, in 1934, where the girls of the title—Doll, Hilary, Amelia, Kathy, and Janet—are high school juniors.

The omniscient narrator's description of their small town as "The Garden City where the Five Great Valleys meet: the Mission, the Missoula, the Blackfoot, the Hellgate, and the Bitterroot," gave me a sense of a place that was shaped, both literally and figuratively, by its geography. There is, of course, geography everywhere, but in Montana, and in the West, generally, I think, geography seems to matter to the people who live there in a way that it doesn't to people living in the Midwest and East. At least it didn't to me, growing up in Detroit, which seemed to my eyes to be a flat, mostly cement-covered area consisting of streets, freeways, and buildings that could have been anywhere. But the sense of a place, the thereness of it, is shaped not only by its geography but also by its inhabitants. And as Savage tracks the changes in the lives of the girls whose story she is telling, she also tracks the changes in the character of the place in which they live—Montana and the American West—as it is "invaded" by those not native to it:

Whoever would have thought that guarded Eden could ever be vulnerable to foreign attack? . . . Everyone knew the real enemy was from the East; few realized that he was already among them, aping their speech and dressing up in their frame of mind.

But in those days the state belonged to those who lived there, and the kids who went to State University came from the state. Now the outsiders come openly, as if they had a perfect right. They come by jet and jalopy from Larchmont and Scranton and Canarsie and from Boston, Massachusetts. They wish to ski while they acquire degrees from the School of Forestry or the School of Mines. Mines! They wouldn't know a mine from a hole in the ground.

The major themes running through *The Girls from the Five Great Valleys* are the terrible inexorability of change (which occurs whether we want it to or not, whether it announces itself loudly or slips in through the back door, unnoticed until it's too late to be prepared) and chance. Change may be inevitable, but how and when it makes itself known to us is unpredictable, often (most often?) to the point of seeming randomness.

Ever since high school, I've kept notebooks (journals, really, with hardboard covers, and the pages sewn in) into which I've copied favorite poems and selections from books and essays. I like to read them over to comfort myself, and to share them with those close to me. Here are some that I chose from *The Girls from the Five Great Valleys*:

Take five girls anywhere, at any time. Three will be all right, and one will make it. One won't.

(Those are the three sentences, coming at the end of the first chapter, that made me realize that this was a book that I'd love.)

And:

> Hilary didn't have everything she wanted. Yet. But she was firm of purpose, kindly, and strong. Weak people are often unhappy; strong people can't take the time. Hilary happened to be very strong.
>
> No credit to her, you understand. That was the way she had been reared.

And:

> That is how Hilary began to learn that up until now she had learned nothing. That no one can afford self-pity, because that most expensive of commodities is always purchased at someone else's cost. And that there is no help at all against the random buffeting of chance.

And:

> In Montana, people kill themselves all the time. They plunge off mountain roads or hit each other head-on, or a cow lumbers up from the barrow-pit, or an antelope. Or they fall asleep at the wheel or hit loose gravel and once in a while, for no apparent reason, a car will just leave the road and sail. Regrettable, of course, but if people are going to maintain those speeds . . . and believe me, people are.

Ultimately, it was the voice of the narrator that kept me reading *The Girls from the Five Great Valleys*, telling me enough, but not too much. Allowing me to use my own imagination, to read between the lines, to enter into my own relationship with the characters. I couldn't resist that voice, and the story it was telling. I couldn't resist spending more time with these girls and learning which one made it and which one didn't, and which three were all right and why and how it all happened the way whatever happened did.

I hope you enjoy *The Girls from the Five Great Valleys* as much as I did.

Nancy Pearl

For Margery Cavanagh

The Girls from the
Five Great Valleys

1

HERE THEY COME.

They have never walked anywhere in their lives: they stride. Their heads are high, but it is not because they remember to hold them high. It is May and school is out and next year they will be women. They will be the best women in town, if Hilary has her way. Hilary usually has her way.

They are crossing the Higgins Avenue Bridge because you have to cross the bridge to get back to the part of town where one lives. The bridge is wide and made of iron; under it the deep brown water coils. There are interesting tales about the bridge. A Miss Gaspard who taught at the high school jumped from it. She lived with her mother and it got too much. The girls are not interested. It was before their time.

They have no money, but it is nineteen thirty-four and nobody in Montana has any money, although some do have less than others. That is why Doll charged the hamburgers to her father. It took a lot of brass to charge anything to her father, but Doll has a lot of brass. She is the prettiest one and she is sly and fun. Sometimes Hilary despairs of making Doll into a better woman.

They have straight backs and taut stomachs and their hair would be nice if they would just let it alone, but only one of them was born here in Missoula. Way up the valley there is a little town, a gas pump and a grocery store and the gray remnants of an Indian mission school that was named for Amelia Lacey's great-grandfather, before he moved to Missoula. Nobody comes from Missoula. Missoula is too new for people to come from. Missoula is a place that people come to.

It is because only one of the girls was born here that Hilary must make the town aware that they are better women. Somebody has to start. Doll knows perfectly well what Hilary is up to. They have been best and dearest friends since second grade. The others have been hand-picked for Hilary's purposes. That is not to say that Hilary does not like each one of them. She likes them very much.

Under the bridge twigs and branches gather. They move nervously and nudge one another until the next surge of brown water sweeps them out. You cannot swim there because the river is too deep and stern. You swim—if you can swim; many mountain people can't—at that place out by Fort Missoula where the river spreads and rests. That's toward the Bitterroot. The Bitterroot Valley is beautiful and deadly. The Indians didn't even fight for it because they knew about the ticks, although they didn't call what happened to you Spotted Fever. When the girls want to hike (everyone hikes around Missoula) their parents say, "Not up the Bitterroot."

Now Hilary stops. When Hilary stops, everybody does. She stops because she sees the boys. They are good-looking boys and they have a car, such as it is. Well, actually, it is a pickup truck. Two of them are on the football team and wear those purple coat-sweaters with the big gold felt *M*'s. The driver, who has black curly hair and a good mouth, Doll knows; he shares a study hall with her and often, as she sits stifling and looking at the clock, she feels him looking at her. Upon this black-haired boy, Doll would not turn her back.

However, Hilary has turned her back. Hilary has not decided yet about these boys. One of them is said to be a rancher's son, but anyone who owns a little land can call himself a rancher. Hilary has not seen the ranch. It may be that the boy's father raises only potatoes or sugar beets. One must be very careful.

Doll agrees that one must be careful, but she does not have the same end in sight. Hilary wishes to be a personage. Doll just wants to get married and get out of her father's house.

Up until now Hilary, by mutual consent, has pretty much managed who they will see and be seen with. They don't care.

They go around in a bunch anyhow and the boys all seem very much alike; they have one thing, especially, in common. Their fathers are all business or professional men and they will all go on to the University, every man Jack. About this, Hilary is very firm. None of them is as attractive as the black-haired boy, but Doll hates farms. Mud and chicken feathers. Ugh. So with the others, she turns away.

But as she turns, Doll has managed to hook her hair back behind one ear and with her mischievous eyes, to catch the level eyes of the black-haired boy. Nobody knows why this gesture is attractive, but it is. Perhaps it is because of the hair itself, which is soft and dark and springs into little curls at her nape and temples. She has a short upper lip, her skin is like an apricot. She is not beautiful; she is the pretty one. Hilary's father, who adores his wife but notices the ladies, says she is cute as a little red wagon.

These boys are not fresh, but they are interested. The girls lean their elbows on the railing of the bridge. Their fannies are firm and cute. The boys give up. They have to. Cars cannot loiter on the bridge.

And then below a dog swings lazily by. His feet are stiff and his belly balloons. He's just your ordinary dog, sort of yellow, and his plumed tail wags with the water. There is a little sandy island down there where things do get caught: beer bottles (everything is legal now), sodden newspapers, cans that glint silver in the sun. The dog bumps against the island. Hilary is reminded of Miss Gaspard.

"Come on," she says. "Let's get going."

They really are nice-looking girls. Their skin is bright. Janet and Kathy and Hilary still use kid curlers, but where they can't get the curlers close enough their hair gleams over a bristle of harsh curls. Their eyes, too, are straight and bright. All things are ahead of them and, in two instances, there are a few things behind them, too.

Yes, they are all fine-looking girls, but only Amelia is beautiful, and she is the one who doesn't care. Now they link arms. They have read somewhere that girls who are best friends do so. Walking abreast that way they take up the whole pavement, but though they are arrogant, they are courteous: if they meet a woman or an older man, they will drop back Indian file. Somehow, they are touching.

Take five girls anywhere, at any time. Three will be all right, and one will make it. One won't.

There they go.

2

Look—it says right here! Campaign: a series of military engagements fought for a known objective over level ground.

Well, the Missoula Valley is not level ground but a scoop in the Rocky Mountains that counts as its own Mounts Jumbo, Sentinel, even Lolo, just across the ridge. However, Hilary had a known objective firmly in mind and no matter what Edna Macpherson thought, it was not to scalp Edna Macpherson. Hilary just wanted her to move over. In her opinion, there was room in Missoula for two better women: she meant to be the other one.

Oh, Missoula in those days—where they lived.

The Garden City where the Five Great Valleys meet: the Mission, the Missoula, the Blackfoot, the Hellgate, and the Bitterroot. Whoever would have thought that guarded Eden could ever be vulnerable to foreign attack? Not Hilary, absorbed as she was in local skirmishes. Everyone knew the real enemy was from the East; few realized that he was already among them, aping their speech and dressing up in their frame of mind.

But in those days the state belonged to those who lived there, and the kids who went to the State University came from the state. Now the outsiders come openly, as if they had a perfect right. They come by jet and by jalopy from Larchmont and Scranton and Canarsie and from Boston, Massachusetts. They wish to ski while they acquire degrees from the School of Forestry or the School of Mines. Mines! They wouldn't know a mine from a hole in the ground.

Back then there wasn't all this traveling around. And if you did propose to cross state lines you went by train, which was fine. Heavy white linens in the dining car and strange black faces. The water stood still in the metal basin while the basin swung.

The nice scary way the couplings clashed and shifted under your feet between Pullman cars (the *Oneida*, the *Hiawatha*, the *Tuxedo Park*). Best of all, through the black empty night, when you squeezed that clasp so that the textured heavy shade went up, to see the mountains scalloped against the sky and far away, the small light in a lonely farm. Perhaps somebody heard you hooting by and envied you—off to Salt Lake City!

Or Ogden or Denver or Seattle, or wherever. Never back again, you bet your boots.

For this very reason, among Hilary's friends it was Kathy who was most suspect, because it was common knowledge that her father came from Pennsylvania and was a scholar—not that many do not think well of scholars, because some do. But scholars don't know anything about carburetors, they can't shoot and they can't fish. And as far as stock is concerned, they don't know which end is up. Besides, if they thought all that much of the man back in Pennsylvania, what was he doing way out here?

And Kathy was a chubby child and supercilious because she knew too much. She could define a vulgarism and did so. Her unpenciled brows would rise if one spoke of a quotation as a quote. Worst of all, she said to know all was to forgive all and she went around forgiving people, which is insulting. It presumes that the forgiver is in a position to forgive.

But Kathy said that was the way she had been reared.

Reared, mind you! All the rest of them were raised.

Hilary's mother had said thoughtfully, "Well, dear, she has a point. That is the correct usage of the word." Then she got up and walked around a little. "Hilary," she said, "have I ever told you that some speak about *the* hoi polloi?"

So after that Kathy and Hilary became friends, and Hilary had no reason to regret it. Kathy had pretty manners and got good grades, which is like having powder in your powder horn. Strong allies help. The only thing—if there was a thing—that was disappointing was that Hilary liked to help and Kathy did not require any help. She was as devious as a spy and Hilary was not always sure that she was not a spy. Sometimes you have to take the chance.

Janet was a strong ally, too.

True, Janet was far from bright, but that was perfectly all right. Lots of people are not one bit interested in brightness. It was more important that her father was a doctor and made a lot of moola. He had been born in a good place—Idaho. Shoup, as a matter of fact, though he preferred to practice in Montana. Well, who wouldn't? Janet had more brushed wool sweaters than anyone in town. She had an amethyst because her birthstone was an amethyst, and she had two rooms of her own, one to sleep in and one in which to keep her own phonograph. By all rights she should have belonged to the enemy, but she didn't. She thought Hilary's bunch was a lot more fun.

And there were ways Hilary could help her. It wasn't easy to get Janet dates because although she had thin pretty yellow hair and had burgeoned, she also had this odd scientific turn of mind.

"What did you mean by that?" she would ask the boys.

The boys didn't like to be asked what they meant by that.

So Hilary was taking her in hand. "Don't ask the fellows," she said. "Ask me what they meant. Besides, your skirt's too short."

And Doll? Oh, Doll! Everyone loved Doll, though there was nothing to be done about her.

But Amelia.

Amelia was the heavy cannon, because Amelia had everything. She had old powerful money, a name mentioned in the archives in Helena (perhaps not flatteringly, but that is not what counts), and the most beautiful mother this side of Hollywood, whom she resembled. Of all of them, she was the one people turned to look at. Even if she had not been good to look at as a blue April morning, people would have looked. Had she been ugly as a tree toad, people would have turned. In Three Forks, in Great Falls, in Billings, someone would have nudged someone. "You see that kid? Her great-granddad was old man Lacey."

But Amelia was shy, frightened, and unhappy.

All of which Hilary meant to change.

It just so happened that she had the power to do it. Some can, some can't. Hilary didn't have everything she wanted. Yet. But she was firm of purpose, kindly, and strong. Weak people often are unhappy; strong people can't take the time. Hilary happened to be very strong.

No credit to her, you understand. That was the way she had been reared.

3

KATHY LIVED OUT by the University, which made sense because her father taught at the University. Janet's father, the doctor, had built out by the Paxson School. Hilary's folks had a comfortable place on Hilda Avenue, and Doll lived over the way.

Amelia lived in the old Lacey mansion.

The old Lacey mansion took up an entire block and was surrounded by a tall iron fence, the shadow of which, in certain lights, lay out against the world like lances. There was an ornamental gate in front and a utilitarian one in back and everyone had keys because the gates were always locked. They had to be.

That was because of the child.

As soon as Amelia left the others she began to hurry and, as always happened when she left Hilary, her confidence seeped away.

She supposed that the hamburgers had been dandy, but she hadn't been able to put her mind to the hamburgers because all day she had been thinking about her mother.

One of the things she appreciated about Hilary was that Hilary understood how rare and precious Amelia's mother was. Very few other people did. Amelia's mother was the loveliest woman in town, except maybe for that girl who had waited tables across from the Great Northern railroad station and later went in the movies. But nobody had known who that girl was. One day she was simply there on the screen. Lo and behold!

Everyone knew who Anne Lacey was and nobody liked her. That was because she made it clear that she did not like them. Anne Lacey was bitterly unhappy in Montana and didn't care who knew. She had been bitterly unhappy ever since Amelia's father died in the wreck on the Hellgate road.

There were some mean enough to say she hadn't been all that happy, even before.

"No!" Amelia protested to Hilary. "It was a love match."

Hilary nodded. She had heard of such. She understood that they were often doomed.

Her own parents seemed to get along, and if they had terrible, interesting problems they didn't let her—or her brother—know. Her brother came in and went out whistling. Hilary's own problems with her mother didn't seem to go far or amount to much and always ended when her mother, challenged, would say, "Give me the old verities!"

Then she would add, "And give me the old soft shoe!" and large as she was, she would start to shuffle around in something that looked more like a cakewalk than the old soft shoe. Once you laugh, it is hard to argue.

Her folks laughed quite a lot and did not seem at all doomed, so perhaps it had not been a love match.

When Will Lacey died he left his wife defenseless and among strangers. Well, not quite defenseless. Just a few nights before he died, Amelia's father came into the room in which Amelia was not sleeping. Downstairs there was a lot of noise and laughter and the Orthophonic kept spinning the same record around and around. Her father was very drunk and very pleasant.

"Honey-bun," he said.

He slouched down on her bed and sank the whole side down. Will Lacey was a large man. She could smell his whiskey and his shaving stuff. She loved him very much. He was always good to her, even when he was sober.

"You and me, honey," he said. "See?"

He breathed heavily, as if he had been running. Besides the whiskey smell, his breath was sort of sick.

"See what I mean?"

Well no, she didn't, but she listened, being used to him. He would make it clear, if he could. If he couldn't she might just as well forget because he would forget, and if she asked in the morning he would shake his head and say with tolerant amusement at his own fuddlement, "I *did*?"

"Because we're the big fellows."

At twelve, Amelia was already two sizes taller than her mother. She had Anne's perfect, delicate features and her black glossy hair and her smoke-colored eyes and slim boneless hands, but Will was right. She was bigger. For some reason, big women often feel responsible. This is not reasonable, but it is so.

Amelia nodded.

"I knew you'd get it. Get it?"

No.

"Take care of them," her father said.

Oh, she would, she would!

He got up then and ambled sort of toward the door and when he had achieved it he leaned his hand on the doorframe and his weight upon his hand.

"You do that," he said. "Honey-bun."

Next week he was dead.

In Montana, people kill themselves all the time. They plunge off mountain roads or hit each other head-on, or a cow lumbers up from the barrow-pit, or an antelope. Or they fall asleep at the wheel or hit loose gravel and once in a while, for no apparent reason, a car will just leave the road and sail. Regrettable, of course, but if people are going to maintain those speeds . . . and believe me, people are.

But since it happened right after the stock market crash, some did wonder if poor Will had lost a lot of the old Lacey money and how much he had lost. None of the Lacey ranches had changed hands, but that didn't mean they weren't mortgaged to the hilt, though nobody from the bank ever said; the bank knew on which side its bread was buttered. Anne Lacey was quite capable of taking all her business elsewhere, and that included everything back East.

And they wondered—Amelia knew because her mother told her—if it had been too much for him. The child. But Amelia knew it had been a true accident. If any kind of a presentiment had made her father speak to her the way he spoke, it was only because he knew as well as the next how much he drank.

Her mother resented his departure very much. From one whose gaiety had been febrile, she turned still and sullen. Oh, not all the time! Sometimes she could be just as sweet! But when it got too much for her, there were certain signs. For one thing, she was irritable in the morning. At these times Amelia might return from school to find Anne locked in her own room. When she was locked in her own room she wouldn't answer. Or else she might be gone for hours, driving her Pierce Arrow like a bat out of hell. That frightened Amelia.

But there were times when she could help, when she could sit and listen while her mother, stretched with one hand across her eyes and her narrow feet with their high arches crossed, talked of the dear times that were gone. Amelia would bring her Fatimas and her tea in an eggshell cup or perhaps just a little gin and, if her head ached, a linen hanky dampened with cologne.

Naturally, Amelia's mother depended on Amelia very much.

"You used to see lots of people," Amelia said.

"Those were your father's friends," her mother told her.

The women, from the start, had been annoyed because Anne had met Will back East and at the Game. It is all right to meet your husband at the Game, but it had better be the West Coast Conference and if everything works out all right (your mother's friends see it works out all right) you had best be a Kappa Kappa Gamma, and he a Phi Delt or an SAE. Either will do.

Anne Lacey had not gone to college, but to one of those swank boarding schools, which she left precipitously when she caught poor Will. And then, she didn't go to Miss Monique's Salon de Beauty, where every single week the women had their hair confined by finger waves. You can't set permanents by yourself; they have to be subdued with sticky lotions that run down your back. There, where they dried under those buckety things, they planned who was going to have the crowd on Saturday. Anne

Lacey wore her black hair straight and bright and shingled, which was so out of date that it was novel. Because of the novelty and the enormous eyes which seemed to promise so much more than she meant, the husbands paid too much attention to her, or had till they decided that she was bad-tempered. Had to be. Hadn't she slapped Harry Osbourne in the pantry? Everyone knew poor Harry never meant anything. Besides, he got his dental degree from Ann Arbor, Michigan. Who did she think she was?

Also, she said idear.

Whoever she thought she was, she didn't send Amelia to dancing school or give birthday parties at which Amelia could meet their children. And it got about that she drank, although she didn't. She drank, that is, but never, never to excess. Excess is bad for the complexion and results in the lowering of guards. Forget it.

Of course everybody drank. It looked kind of funny if you didn't. For years they had all shared the same bootlegger, and even if you hadn't tied one on it sounded better on Monday morning to say, "Boy, did I tie one on." Friendlier. But drinking was not to interfere with your bridge game or your golf, and you were not supposed to sit on a midweek morning with gin in your orange juice beside your swimming pool. In fact, you were not supposed to have a swimming pool. What was the matter with the one at the Country Club?

But not many drank the way Will Lacey used to drink. He probably wouldn't have if he had married one of them, and it all came from sending kids back East to school, where they were bound to meet those who did not suit.

They assumed she had married him because of all that Lacey money, but about that they were also wrong. Anne's own father had had a lot of money, though it was not generally known around Missoula, and not much stock would have been put in it anyway. You never know about out-of-state money; how can one be sure? While everybody knew about the Lacey money. Will's grandfather had been disbarred for throwing bribes over transoms in that Butte hotel at the time when W.A. Clark was trying to buy a Senate seat. That was during the War of the Copper Kings. Montanans don't like to be reminded of it very much. If people are crazy enough to dig up stuff like that and print it, why don't they look at the history of their own states?

Anyway, it was too bad that a Lacey had been caught, but it turned out all right because W.A. Clark was a loyal man in a cold way and had given Will's grandfather a tidy sum to make up. With what was left of the tidy sum Will's father made some shrewd investments and bought up properties all over the state. Poor Will himself had never done much of anything except to drive around in that Stutz and look at the properties. Perhaps he had not yet got going.

Amelia would have been a shy child anyway, and after her father died, her mother wanted her home all the time.

"I can't rattle around here by myself," she said.

So while the other girls clanged round on the Giant Strides and kissed the boys in the basement, Amelia came straight home. There was no need for that. If Anne had been willing to weep on the shoulders of just two women and then give a little dinner party, all would have been forgiven.

Well, she wasn't willing.

That's why until Amelia went to high school and met Hilary, she didn't know she had potential. That's what Hilary told her, that she had potential. She looked up one day in Algebra and here was this tall redheaded girl looking at her. And when Algebra was dismissed this girl was waiting for her at the door and she said, "Pardon me, but you don't wear your makeup right. However, I believe you have potential."

And in the next few weeks Hilary showed her why Tangee was more subtle and how to keep the outline of her lips—powder them first is the trick. And how to snub the boys if they were not the boys from whom you wished attention.

Although frankly and honestly, and beautiful as she was, the boys were not drawn to Amelia. They looked at her great smoky eyes and at the long gleaming hair that she did not put up, and then they ran like hell. Hilary fixed up dates for her and her mother bought her clothes (about clothes, Anne was not penurious), but when someone started French-kissing in the pantry, nobody ever kissed Amelia.

"You scare them off," Hilary tried to tell her.

"From what?" asked Amelia.

There you had it.

4

AT FIRST, ANNE DID NOT care for Hilary. "I don't know who she is," she said.

Then on an awful day Anne found Hilary's note in Amelia's jacket pocket. "You take Wilson," the note said. "I'll take George."

What is a mother supposed to make of that?

As it happened, the note referred only to a Rainbow dance. Hilary's mother was an Eastern Star, so Hilary was a Rainbow girl. The Eastern Stars didn't care who came as long as the youngsters had a wholesome time and there was enough left to pay the orchestra. Then too, Anne soon discovered that Hilary was quite as selective as she was herself. Hilary's admiration of her friend's mother was intense. Nobody minds being admired intensely.

Hilary couldn't understand why there weren't men around Anne all the time. Amelia could have told her. Her mother didn't like the men any more than she liked women. They had no élan and proved expensive. Even before the Depression frightened her, she had not been much for entertaining, and she discouraged those of Will's friends who had dropped around at first to offer sympathy and support. Anne said she was tired of running a free bar.

Seeing her mother's dissatisfaction and her restlessness, Amelia once asked, "Why don't we go back East?"

But Anne's parents were dead and both the big place in Brookline and the summer place in Magnolia sold long ago. To tell the truth, she had not had many friends back there. Much as she disliked the West, there was no reason to go East.

So when Amelia asked, Anne nibbled at a pale pink shell of nail and said, "Who would take this pile off my hands?"

Nobody wanted those big places any more except fraternities and clinics. And the old Lacey mansion always had been gloomy. It had brown shingled turrets and cupolas and eaves and a huge brown porch on which, in the wintertime, the dry hop vines shook. Wet rotting leaves were soggy under the bushes; even on sunny days the tall blue spruces seemed to drip and underneath, a rug of needles was porous as a sponge. Out back, there was a carriage house where Will had kept his Stutz, the one he died in, and where now Anne kept the Pierce Arrow and, for Amelia, the little tan Chevvy. There were rooms up above where Spud lived.

Amelia headed first around that way because she needed to see him. Next to her, he was the one who understood.

Spud was the only one left of what her father used to call "the help" and her mother, "the staff." Well, there was Mrs. Phelps, but Mrs. Phelps did not live in. Mrs. Phelps had a pink crimped face and crimped iron-colored hair; she sighed a lot. About Amelia's mother she said, "It takes everybody different." Mrs. Phelps was a widow herself. Then she would add with cold satisfaction, "But Mrs. Lacey's not the first to lose a good man. Nor she won't be the last."

Herself, Mrs. Phelps missed the parties. She had liked to watch the young people acting up and then later tell her friends how they acted. Like when the ladies saddled the gentlemen and rode them all around the living room. She missed the way the big rooms blazed with light and the way the fringe flew on the dresses and the beads rattled and winked. And like as not before the night was through they would all pile into those big cars and go tarry-hooting off somewhere to see the sun rise or have breakfast with their bootlegger. Who minded then if the help helped themselves?

Spud and Mrs. Phelps didn't get along too well. They both felt they had too much to do, and they were right. Today, for instance, Spud was sitting outside the carriage house in a warm patch of sun polishing shoes. That was okay—good!—he wouldn't expect Mrs. Phelps to polish shoes. But she wouldn't polish anything. Spud had to do the furniture, the mirrors, the massive coffee urn, and the epergnes and candelabra. Mrs. Phelps drew the line. She cleaned and cleared and scrubbed and, as she pointed out, she did these thorough, but she wouldn't polish and she wouldn't cook.

Spud got awfully sick of cooking.

"We used to have all the help we could use," he grumbled. "The windows all want to be washed."

Mrs. Phelps would say doubtfully, "I can see can I get my niece."

Both of them had to watch the child.

"I have to let things go," Spud said. "I can't keep up."

Anne Lacey said with sweet regret, "Then I may have to find someone who can."

The minute that Amelia saw Spud there in the sun she slowed down. If anything bad had happened, he wouldn't just be sitting there.

The worst of it was that Amelia was never sure of what bad thing she was afraid. She was afraid of her mother's silence and of her recklessness. She might be lying in a darkened room with her eyes fixed on the ceiling, planning something desperate. But what? It is true that she had once said to Amelia, "Oh, what's the use?" How Amelia's heart had pounded. Up at the cottage at the lake there was a gun, and anyone can get hold of razors. And, with a little difficulty, she supposed sleeping pills. But it was the Pierce Arrow of which she thought most often.

Amelia said, "Is everything all right?"

Spud was a dry, wry person, jockey-sized. He spit into the shoe polish, rubbed his cloth, raised a shoe and looked at it critically. It happened to be one of Amelia's, with a round toe and a needle heel.

"Ruin your feet," he said. "Of course everything's all right. She went downtown but she came back. Honest to God, Amelia, stop worrying, or you won't make old bones."

Sometimes Amelia wished that her mother did drink, which you could at least get your hands on.

"Bunions," Spud said.

Nobody knew where Spud came from unless her mother knew. He had once told Amelia that he had been her father's batman in the war. And it was true that he used to sing to her:

Farmer, have you a daughter fair
Who can wash a soldier's underwear?

But Americans don't have batmen. They have buddies.

Then he said he had met her father on the border when they had both been after old Juárez. That was just silly. Then he said he had been a cowboy on a Lacey ranch. He did look tough and ropy enough for that and he had a limp—a horse, he said, had fallen with him in an arroyo. But in Montana they aren't called arroyos. Amelia would look at him levelly and he would look right back.

All right, her mother was all right. But what about the child?

Spud said, "She's napping, and you needn't think I haven't checked."

Somebody had to check. The child hid in closets where she could suffocate and she hid in bathtubs where she could drown. She could cut herself or fall and Spud was supposed to see she didn't, but Spud couldn't be everywhere at once, and so it was Amelia who had had to burn her.

Nobody loved the child: couldn't. In all honesty, there was nothing there to love. She was born the year before her father died and, for the first year, Anne hadn't noticed. What is there to notice when a child isn't even one year old? Naturally, after Will died Anne was distracted. You would have thought somebody would have noticed, but if they did they didn't say. But by the time she was three, everyone noticed.

Unfortunately, the child wasn't pretty. She was pinch-featured, small for her age, her no-colored hair had never thickened. She bit her nails until they were fat lumps buried in inflamed fingertips. She was afraid of everyone. But worst of all, the frail body was active as a fly. Because she didn't love the child, Amelia was anguished. And yet that day, somebody had to burn her.

Amelia came in after school. Anne slept a lot to get through the days; she must have been asleep or else she would have smelled the smoke. The child still slept in a crib; that was the first time they knew she could get out of it. The smoke came from what would have been the guest room, if Anne ever had any guests. The door was closed . . . if the child had locked it. But the heavy door swung at her touch and in the draft from the open window the filmy curtains reached for the dancing light of the burning newspapers, and the child laughed.

Amelia pulled her free and beat the papers into sour cinders while her heart knocked with hope. That a match makes a pretty light is a concept and the child had grasped it. But the child had no concept of pain.

And so, for the most painful moment of her life, Amelia held her little sister's hand in the flame of another match.

The child didn't hold any grudge; she had no memory for grudges. She never lit a match again, either, but that might well have been simply that she forgot matches. What hurt Amelia was that after that the child cowered before her the way a gentle and affectionate dog will cower.

When she had to tell somebody, she told Spud. She said, "Don't say anything to my mother."

Spud said, "Do you think I'm nuts?"

5

WELL, NATURALLY, Hilary was fascinated.

Here was this lost lovely lonely woman who knew so much that she herself would love to know. And her wild gentle daughter who would be a lot better off if she knew a few things that Hilary happened to know. And this eccentric old withered man who was a poet, when he was in the mood.

"Spud," Hilary would beg. "Sing it again."

> Keep your head down, Fritzi boy. . . .

"Do it again."

> You were mending the broken wire
> When we opened rapid fire. . . .

And we won't be back until it's over over there!
A lot, lot later Hilary found herself responding to other cadences.

> We'll hang out our laundry on the Siegfried Line
> If the Siegfried Line's still there.

It made her just as cross as she could be. But no matter how much she might disapprove, there went the old blood trilling.

> It was he who drew the fire of the enemy
> That a company of men might live to fight. . . .

Allons, enfants de la Patrie . . .

Rule, Britannia, Britannia rules the waves!

Hilary couldn't see how you are going to get the lion and the lamb into cahoots when the very child who should lead them stands beside his desk and pipes, heart swelling and banging in the skinny breast,

> He is trampling out the vintage where the grapes of wrath
> are stored. . . .

Even in the second grade you can see through that.

> He has loosed the fateful lightning of his terrible
> swift sword!

Poets, Hilary thought, have a lot to account for.

Hilary Hunter was seven years old and ready for the second grade when they moved down from Polson because her father was sick to death of Polson.

Missoula was pretty scary.

First she learned to get to the Roosevelt School by her own self and then she learned to make tiny combs by sticking broom straws into clay. And then she learned that the better girls go to the Paxson School.

Out by the Paxson School the houses were all new and it was rumored that they had two baths up and one bath down. And out there the grass was new and sparse, whereas around the house her father bought on Hilda Avenue the grass was rich and tall and ragged until her father got after it.

In Polson, Hank Hunter had tried coal. But around Polson there are not that many people who need coal. On the one hand you have your Flathead Indians, and, on the other, the Bison Range and in between are tourists, who do not require much coal.

Polson scatters for a short way along Flathead Lake, the larg
est body of water, Montanans like to have you know, in these
United States, if you don't count the Great Lakes or the Great
Salt Lake, which is suspect because it is salt. The streams that
seep or tumble into Flathead come from Glacier Park and from
ranges no one has yet named because they are too formidable and
no one has yet been there.

Nevertheless, when the Hunters lived there, a lot of the east
shore was cultivated. Cherry orchards. The west coast was the best
coast, timbered with tamarack and deep with shade and nothing at all between Polson and Kalispell. In those days if you ran
out of gas, you were out. And not the worst thing, either. What
is the matter with walking? Walking, you see the shadow of a
needle shift, and a striped sudden chipmunk scuffs the dust and
regards you soberly before he decides that after all, he might as
well mosey along.

But Hilary had a lot against Flathead, where her father had
not sold much coal. For one thing, it was no longer fashionable
because of the tourists and the cherry trade. For another, between
here and there are miles and miles of total emptiness where—she
kept trying to explain to Doll—a boy could stop a car. The point
was that whether the boy stopped the car or not, there was no
way to prove he hadn't. Also her father wouldn't let her drive up
Flathead way because he said, what if she got a flat?

Hilary preferred Little Bear Lake.

You may not go to Little Bear unless you own, and the better
families who own are old and few. Little Bear is small and wild.
At night the mountain lions whine and the loons cry. You have
to pack in everything and keep your milk in the cold shallows of
the lake. There is a store on the east side but you can't get there,
unless you take your boat.

You would think people who could afford would rather be
someplace where they could use their Kelvinator, but that is not
the way it works. There was no electricity at Little Bear except

across the lake where the people who ran the store had a wind-charger. Who wants a wind-charger?

People who can afford prefer to pretend to be hard up. They like Coleman lanterns and bumpy mattresses and having to go outside.

The Laceys had had a place at Little Bear forever; it was to Hilary just another proof that her friend's family ranked high. Every place has a list where some rank high. Sometimes it is topped by oil and sometimes by stocks and sometimes by antiquity, if in a hundred years it is possible to become antique. You know how in ancient desiccated valleys one may see, horizontally striping the flanks of foothills, each layer of silt as it rained down and settled in the old waters? So in Montana:

The first settlers. Those who made the money.

Ranchers. They may hawk at the table, but they own the land.

The educators and educated. Many are suspect.

Small businessmen.

Those who clerk for small businessmen.

Riffraff.

In Missoula, as elsewhere, there is a good deal of downward mobility; almost none up. But up was where Hilary meant to be, and up was where she felt that she belonged. Her forebears were from the South, a point in her favor. So many fine, fine men came west after—or during—the Civil War. Unfortunately, her mother's family had settled in the bare baked land around Miles City and had not even tried to raise wheat, but were teachers and ministers and such.

Nobody ever spoke about her father's side.

But while her claim to come from the best first settlers was dubious, she could ally herself with those who could so claim.

And if it came to that, she could turn Episcopalian.

6

AFTER THEY CROSSED the bridge and headed toward the University, there were no more stores. That is why it was the better part of town. Over there, you had your hustlers and your cockfights. Over here, you had your pride. There was never an Indian seen on this side of town.

Of course some parts of the better part of town are better. On the whole, from Higgins Avenue it is better to turn left than to turn right. Today, just before they got to Missoula County High, Janet and Kathy and Amelia were going to turn left, and Doll and Hilary right. That is, if Hilary could not prevent it.

"Where'll we go?" she asked. "Doll's?"

Doll's was best because her mother was dead and there was no one home all day.

"No siree-bob," Doll said. "As it is, I'm going to get my rump thumped."

That is the sort of thing Hilary wished Doll wouldn't say. Doll had no one except her father, who was mean, and her brother, who was even meaner, so you couldn't hold her responsible. However, she was not going to be a lot of help on the way up.

Naturally Hilary was disappointed, but if they had to separate, they had to. And it was just as well, because right ahead of them and coming down the broad stone steps of the high school was one of her favorite people in the world.

Mr. Barry.

You can't get anywhere in Missoula—not anywhere that counts—without passing Missoula County High. It's that big yellow brick building that takes up the whole block between Higgins and Gerald Avenue. There used to be an apron of grass on one end, but that was before the fire. The fire broke out late at night, but everybody came. If there was no one home to be with the kids, they brought the kids.

Anyone would wish to see the high school burn.

All that year while the old building was being repaired and the annex started, classes were held at the University. The regents had to permit. There was already enough trouble between town and gown. Hilary loved it. She found it educational. Coming and going that year in her longer skirt, because that year they were longer, and jodhpur boots—for some reason they were all wearing jodhpur boots—Hilary began to understand that there were better women all over the state, and that they gathered at the Kappa Kappa Gamma House.

Or at the Delta Gammas' or the Chi Omegas.' But if you look older than your age, who is to know that you are not a Chi Omega?

Those big pillared fraternity and sorority houses along University Avenue looked a lot different to her now than they had looked when she and Doll were in fourth grade. Back in fourth they used to skate up and around the Oval (pausing to swing around the flagpole in front of Main Hall) and then back past the white and sumptuous houses where the busy young women paid no attention to them but the young men, lounging upon their several steps, would tease them in a friendly way and even, if your skate were loose or you could arrange to loosen them, would take your key and tighten them for you.

For a long time after they gave up roller skates they still liked to put one hand on the cool, smooth pole and swing around it.

This year, Hilary wouldn't be caught dead.

Seeing them, Mr. Barry waited. Mr. Barry was Hilary's friend, neighbor, and teacher, a gentle, bristling man with bruised dark eyes who looked a lot like Walt Disney and lived next door to Doll. He lived in a bungalow because on Hilda most of the houses were bungalows; Hilary's house was two-story, but then, her father owned. Most rented. It was well known that Mr. Barry rented, but he kept the grass watered, and everyone knows that teachers have to rent.

Mr. Barry lived in his bungalow with a frightened pleasant wife of whom Hilary's mother thought the world, and a nice little boy. Hilary had liked Mr. Barry even while she still went to the Roosevelt and didn't realize he was a teacher because he didn't teach at the Roosevelt. He was the kind of neighbor who let you come on over to get your ball.

This year Hilary took his course. There were two sections of P.A.D., which meant Problems of American Democracy. (More people should have had to take it.) Hilary wanted Mr. Barry's section because, as she said, better the devil she knew to the devil she didn't.

Her mother said in the soft voice she used because *her* mother had said a low voice was an excellent thing in woman, "But Hilary. That wasn't exactly what I meant by that old saying."

"Well, then," Hilary said, "what did you mean?"

It wasn't easy to get into Mr. Barry's class because his class wasn't dull. The other section was in the fragile hands of a pretty woman with a long pink nose, who wept when the boys acted up and had much, much too much to say about James Polk. She approached all problems timidly as if, if it were not for her forbearance, they might go away. Only once—deeply stirred—had she raised a shell-nailed hand and cried out cautiously, "Tippecanoe, and Tyler, too!" Later she married a sociologist and never in her life had anything more to do with the Missoula County High School.

Whereas Mr. Barry talked about Anaconda Copper. He said that Anaconda owned the banks and the judges and the newspapers and the senators and the Board of Regents.

Well, everyone knew that, though most did not mention it.

And Mr. Barry did other things that were not wise. He wore a hat. To this day in the Garden City Where the Five Great Valleys Meet, men wear hats. But proper hats. Proper hats are Stetsons. They don't make Stetsons anymore, but Monkey Ward makes a sort of Stetson and so does J.C. Penney. That kind of hat indicates that though you may not be a rancher, you live near where the ranchers live and have in mind the welfare of the West.

Mr. Barry's hat had a narrow brim. He said it was a Borsolino and he said it was the finest hat ever made. His wife had given it to him for Christmas and after the holidays he showed his class how you could jump up and down on it and it still came back in shape.

But it was an odd hat to wear in the Garden City.

That afternoon Hilary could tell by the set of the Borsolino that he had talked about Anaconda Copper once too often. Most of the parents did not like to talk about Anaconda and they didn't like anyone to talk about Anaconda to their young, because there it was and there you were and who can tell?

"Well, kids," Mr. Barry said when Hilary and Doll caught up, "how's tricks?"

Hilary didn't bother to answer because it was perfectly obvious how tricks were.

Mr. Barry could not be said to walk; he sauntered. Doll had no time to saunter. She was supposed to turn her father's bedroom out, and it was bad enough not to have done it, not to mention hamburgers. But Hilary couldn't help her much about the bedroom. She could shake sheets with the best of them but she didn't know what to do about his underwear and frankly and honestly didn't care to know.

So she handed Doll her canvas notebook and her geometry and said, "I'll get them later."

Doll hooked her soft dark hair behind her ear and said, "OK, kid-do." Then she danced across Higgins Avenue.

"Doll has a sort of a problem at home," Hilary explained.

Mr. Barry said, "Yes, I know."

Hilary said, "I don't just mean today."

Mr. Barry said, "Yes. I know."

"She certainly is one pretty kid," he said with very little interest.

They watched Doll take the shortcut through the alley in back of the University apartments. That was a long, low building with gray granite porches in front and kidney-colored brick in back— in that alley the very first boy who ever kissed Hilary had kissed her and she hadn't minded one bit. He did, though. He gave her a dime-store ring and a week later had to ask her to give it back because it was his sister's dime-store ring. Bud Worden.

If you did not take the shortcut but went openly to the corner of Higgins and Hilda, the next house you passed had once belonged to a professor of Mathematics.

The professor was not well liked in town, because he had more money than was suitable for one who was, when you got right down to it, just a teacher. For all their black gowns and their funny hats that's all they are, just teachers, and only bearable because they have less money than most. While this man, with a series of workbooks, had made a pile. No matter what their fathers thought, the children had to buy them. Teacher said. Later he married a firm gray person who moved him to a big new house out by the Paxson School. She felt it was more suitable.

With one hand Mr. Barry swung a faded green sort of sack. He carried test papers in that sack and, when it rained, his rubbers. That wasn't liked much, either. It looked funny. Somebody said that back at Harvard everyone carried those sacks. Maybe so. Out here, it looks funny. With his free hand Mr. Barry rattled a pencil along the palings of the picket fence. At the end of the fence he swung about and pointed the pencil at Hilary.

"Bang," he said. "They got me, pal."

And then he staggered and pretended he was going to fall.

He was thirty-five if he was a day.

Hilary was not going to pretend. She didn't think it was fair to his wife.

Then Mr. Barry didn't pretend any more. He scuffed along with his hands in his pockets. The dubious bag knocked at his knee.

He said, "Contracts came out. Oh yes-siree, I got one. But Mr. Gilpin says take this year to look around."

That year if you were told to look around you felt the wind cold at your nape. He watched his shoes as carefully as if they might take off in some wrong direction. He said, "I wonder why."

Hilary began to see why his wife was nervous. Older people are not supposed to ask questions of the young. It isn't fair. Besides, when you are older, you are supposed to know. Of course nobody likes to be told to look around. Look around *where?*

Mr. Barry said, "I thought the kids liked me."

Hilary was swept with rage, because she liked him and most of the kids liked him (though not all), but he should not dump it on her. Of course the kids liked him, because he was honest, and he didn't take his tempers out on them. But kids don't count. Those who have bank accounts resent having their young taught to question the bank accounts: they are the ones who count.

However, if he really wanted to know, Hilary could tell him. For a principal, Mr. Gilpin was a decent man, but he had a nervous wife, too. Hilary didn't know where to begin, since you are not encouraged to advise your elders. They don't like it. One of the things that Mr. Barry ought not to do was to talk to her as if she was a person. Teachers are not supposed to talk to students, not as if they are persons.

On the other hand, she did like his wife, and her own mother, who was a sterling judge of character, liked Mrs. Barry, too. If someone didn't tell him what he was doing wrong, then when he got another job (if he did get another job) he would go right on doing what he was doing that was wrong.

"Hilary," Mr. Barry said, "What am I doing wrong?"

Well, then.

That spring (because of her kid curlers) Hilary's hair looked rather like a dandelion and when she swung her head her hair didn't swing. By next fall, she would know better. She turned and said, "The kids do like you. Most of them."

That was not what he wanted her to say. He thrust his hands deeper in his pockets. He wanted her to say, "*All* the kids like you."

"Which kids?" he asked.

Unfortunately, the wrong ones.

She said, "Well, me. I think what you say is interesting."

He said, "Oh, God."

"I mean it," she said honestly. "I mean I never thought before about how awful everybody is."

"Oh, God," he said.

"Mostly," she told him, "folks don't talk that way."

They crossed Higgins silently. She was almost as tall as Mr. Barry was. Hilary was a tall girl.

He said, "In what way should I not talk?"

Already it was even harder than she had thought. He was demanding that she define, which is what makes a good teacher so tiring.

She said, "A couple of weeks ago? You said Anaconda had raped the state? And the fellows snickered?"

Mr. Barry struck his brow. He said, "Of all the ugly words . . . !"

"Yes," she agreed. "However, they do snicker."

It is strange, but on the right of Higgins Avenue there are no trees. Well, there are not *no* trees. But barring your occasional maple or quaking aspen, there are few trees. The street where Hilary and Mr. Barry lived was bald. And the big brown hills that hump around the Garden City are bare as a baby's bottom. Some who are loyal claim that Missoula is above the timberline. That is not so. True, by the riverbank there are places where the shade shifts easily in June and the light is green and the leaf-shadow dapples the brown water. But the wrong people live down there, sandwiched between the Great Northern and the Milwaukee.

It is no wonder that Hilda Avenue appreciates people who produce petunias. Little Mrs. Barry had tried very hard with morning glories, but they had not taken hold. Her petunias were somewhat better and Hilary commented upon them warmly, but Mr. Barry was not to be diverted.

He said, "Your father's a good man. What does he think about the way I talk?"

Sometimes it is not comfortable to tell the truth. But Hilary's mother, when young, had taken elocution, and she still liked to hold her long hands up and to declaim:

> Oh, what a tangled web we weave
> When first we practise to deceive!

There was another that the girls begged for.

> Would that every fair girl in this drink-laden land
> Would say, "I'll never give my heart—nor my hand—

And here she would touch her heart and extend her hand,

> "To one whom I have reason to think
> Would touch one drop of that vile cursed drink,"
> But would say—when wooed—"I'm a foe to the vine!
> And the lips that touch liquor shall never touch mine!"

Then she would giggle.

What a nice woman.

At any rate, as far as it was practical, Hilary did try to tell the truth, because being caught in a tangled web does not work to one's advantage.

She said now, "I don't know what my father thinks. I think he thinks it's better for me not to know."

Mr. Barry sounded hurt. He said, "Well, then, tell who doesn't like me."

Hilary said, "Edna Macpherson doesn't."

"You mean that fat pale little girl?"

That was who she meant.

Mr. Barry not only took out after the Copper Kings like a terrier at the heels of a big boy, but once in awhile got after the Cattle Barons and took a swipe at Wall Street. But mostly he came back to Butte, which was, he said, an economic Sodom (his bruised eyes would light with the fun of it) and Gomorrah.

And he mentioned names and not only mentioned them but dwelt upon them. Clark. Daly. Heinze. Lacey. And he said that in Montana, which was a part of the Louisiana Purchase and wasn't even a state until 1889, the banks had been camp followers.

Now Edna Macpherson's father was the bank, and her great-great-grandmother was a Heinze. Not *that* Heinze, but connected, and while *that* Heinze stayed in Butte robbing everybody blind, *this* Heinze opened the Emporium, where they still robbed you blind.

To be fair, Hilary could see why Edna didn't care to listen to all that.

And what—pray tell—was wrong with the Emporium? When folks were pushing west they needed flour and needles and to this present day people need needles. And clothing and hardware and fancy groceries like bottled mushrooms and all sorts of things you don't find at the A&P. There's nothing wrong with the Emporium.

No! The Macphersons were just simple honest folk who happened to get here first; Missoula is proud of them. Even now on Pioneer Day (it used to be great sport to fine those too finicky to grow beards—but beards are not so much fun anymore) the Emporium displays the cracked brown daguerreotypes of the Macphersons and the Heinzes standing sternly in front of what at the time was just a trading post where they accommodated people hot to get on to the coast and those few Indians who from time to time required to trade.

By the time the post opened most of the Indians had been forced away, although Chief Joseph was yet to lead his people through the Bitterroot and up through the Beaverhead, mile by bloody mile. You may remember what happened to Chief Joseph.

It was too bad, because all they wanted to do was to leave. They had hoped to get to Canada while they still had a few children left.

Naturally, they were not allowed.

The first Macpherson had nothing to do with that retreat. In the daguerreotype he stands on the baked earth before the splintered veranda of his store looking frugal; he doesn't look like one who would have tangled with Chief Joseph. Why should he? While you are building a business, others had better do the tangling. Indians use flour too and their women use needles, and an Indian is just as good as the next.

Back in those days the famous Higgins Avenue Bridge did not exist and there was nothing on this side of the river. The University (with that unfortunate statue of the Grizzly Bear) is Johnny-come-lately. One wonders where Mr. Macpherson and she whose maiden name was Heinze slept. They must have had a room out back. In the old picture she looks pleasant and intimidated. His great-great-granddaughter looks like him. Of course if you are the first person to get to wherever it is you got to, you are better than other people, because you got there first.

Mr. Barry happened upon a nice rock. It was flat on the bottom (though rounded on the top) so that it skidded well. He kicked it. When they had walked on a few steps, he kicked it again.

Upon the day that Hilary had mentioned, Mr. Barry might just as well have come right out and said that Edna Macpherson's ancestors were gangsters. You don't have to be crazy about your ancestors to prefer that they should not be called gangsters. And Mr. Barry said that anyone high up in the Anaconda was a murderer. While it is perfectly true that Clark and Daly arranged warfare underground, why not call them generals?

But Mr. Barry said it was the same thing.

And he said that the men who died underground—falling timbers, noxious gases, explosions, foes—made the St. Valentine's Day massacre look like a picnic.

Edna Macpherson yawned. Hilary saw her yawn. Then she turned in her seat to look at her best friend. Her best friend's blonde brows rose, and her plump shoulders. The threat was unmistakable and while she knew it was unwholesome, Hilary was interested. She had never before seen anybody threatened.

Now she said, "Mr. Barry. Edna Macpherson? On her mother's side? Heinzes?"

"Oh?" Mr. Barry said. Then he said, "Oh."

The Barrys' little house was spanking clean, but shabby. They had painted, but by now the old new paint bumped on the kitchen cabinets and the new paper with the cabbage roses had faded. But everything that could be washed was washed and all the windows sparkled. Hilary's mother was of the opinion that you could tell a lot about people by their windows; she said Mrs. Barry should be proud.

Hilary asked, "So what'll you do now?"

"Look around," he said bitterly. And then he said, "Don't mention it to her. She liked it here."

Mr. Barry picked up his stone with the obvious intention of scaling it away. He looked at it. And then he put it in his pocket.

"Well," Hilary said. This was not easy. "I know you think a lot of what you think is true."

His dark eyes glowed the way they always did when he was either interested or angry.

Words can be hard to find if you are talking about something to which you haven't given much thought. True, Hilary attended Problems of American Democracy; she hadn't given much thought to the Problems.

She said, "But Mr. Barry. Edna thinks that what she thinks is true."

He said, "Well, she's wrong."

"Besides," Hilary said, "if everyone went around saying just anything they wanted? Also," she said, "if Edna thinks you're wrong, for her you're wrong and for her, she's right."

"My God," he said. "A relativist."

There you were. That was the kind of thing he knew. But by and large, she thought that what she knew was more useful. Make friends, not enemies, but be careful. Because the wrong friend can do a lot of damage, while the right enemy can be used. But there was no sense in trying to teach Mr. Barry this sort of thing. It was not within his scope.

"Listen," she tried, "if you were teaching in Salt Lake, would you go all around saying how awful Mormons are?"

His eyes were bright as a boy's.

"No," he said. "Because they're not awful. Some things, like their underwear, are silly. But leave the Garments out; you can tell a Mormon town because a Mormon town is clean, and they take care of their own."

It hadn't been a good example she had chosen.

"But in Utah, no one would mind what you said about Montana Power?"

"I only say what's true. That I'll say anywhere."

There wasn't much she could do for Mr. Barry.

His nice little wife came out upon their porch where the morning glories had not done very well.

"Sssh," Mr. Barry said.

Hilary dropped her voice. "Anyway," she said, "if I were you I wouldn't sit on top of your desk. It looks funny."

Hilary crossed the street to her own house, and walked about the house to the backyard, where there were, each in its own good time, zinnias, peonies, and nasturtiums. Her father's truck stood in the alley and her father stood with his hands on his hips and looked critically at the flowerbeds. *His* flowerbeds. Everything outside the house belonged to him. Everything inside belonged to Myra. That seemed fair.

Hank Hunter was a red man, tall, on the swaggering side. He was not exactly handsome, though most people thought he was. Ladies, that is. Everyone knew he had a temper, but no one seemed to mind it much; in his own household they had pretty much learned to step around it. Hilary's younger brother achieved this by never being home. Dan was a Boy Scout and camped out a lot. Wherever a team of anything was formed, Dan was on it. He belonged to a group that met at other boys' houses (but not his own) to put ham radios together and then use them. He had a paper route.

This is not to say Dan didn't like his father. He did. He thought the world of him. He just thought it was better not to be around too much.

Naturally Myra Hunter adored Dan. He was her son. But she had more fun with Hilary.

In between tempers, Hilary liked her father a whole lot. He had a nifty sense of humor and in a rough sort of way was good company. When she saw her father on the street, which she often did because he spent his time delivering coal in the wintertime, and ice in the summer, she liked the idea of him. He had a long stride and held his shoulders straight. She did wish he would wear a jacket, but when she became one of Missoula's best, she would see that he wore a jacket. And she wished his name was not Hank, although Hank was the very name for him. Meantime she shared with her mother the comfortable illusion that there was nothing he couldn't do.

Except to join the Country Club.

Hilary's mother was First Families of Virginia—well, not really, but she had kin back here. She sometimes said, looking up from her old black piano, "Child, you *belong*." It was just a matter of making Missoula see it.

Hank's people had come from Virginia, too, but with a difference. *West* Virginia.

"In that line of the family," Hilary's mother said, "they were all decent people."

Hilary went to her father for practical advice and to her mother for moral advice. Mr. Barry's problem promised to involve both, and her father was available. However, he was frowning at the beds where the zinnias and nasturtiums and the peonies were going to be. Best of all, probably, but Myra would not have their huge mop-heads in the house because of the ants. Peonies have to have ants to propagate. Any fool knows that. Yes, Myra said, but that does not make ants any more attractive.

The trouble was that Dan was supposed to keep the beds damp and the beds were dry. Hank crumpled a sod with the heel of his boot.

"What's up, Dad?" she asked.

"Mind your own business," he said, but absently.

Hilary was never as reluctant to push her father as Dan was, perhaps because she was the girl and perhaps because she had her father's foxy hair. "It rained just a while ago," she said. "I shouldn't think you'd want to get all steamed up."

The color started at his cheekbones and brimmed up until you could hardly see the line between his forehead and his rusted hair. He had gone straight from phase one, simple annoyance, to phase three.

"Mind your own business!" he shouted.

So Hilary thought she would.

The kitchen was immaculate in an easygoing way, and was flooded with soft yellow sun. On the floor there were quiet-colored braided rugs that Myra's own mother had made before her eyes went bad. The rugs were so arranged that nobody had to step on them.

Between the living room and the dining room there was an arrangement that would later fall out of fashion and still later reappear as a divider. On one side of this Myra kept the framed picture of herself at the Eastern Star convention in Helena that time. On the other side were the family photographs. It would have been a nice place for plants, but it was too dark for plants.

The plants were in the dining room in a big bay window where the sun could reach the snake cactus and the begonias, but nothing else. Sun fades things.

It should have been a gloomy house. It wasn't. In summer it was cool, in winter, cozy as a cave. Summer and winter, it smelled of good food. Myra and Hank shared a passionate regard for good food. Other women's kitchens smell of cleaning agents: Sapolio and Fels-Naptha. Myra's kitchen smelled of spice and apples, of blackstrap molasses and vanilla and yeast. Pies stood tiered on racks in the pantry, rolls cooled in great bright pans, and the last roast invited the carving knife even while the new roast roasted.

This had had little or no effect on Hank (he was a long-muscled and hard-bellied man). Unfortunately, Myra had grown stout. One would prefer to say plump, because she had such a pretty face; cheeks soft and flushed as a tea-rose and thick lashes that veiled her dark eyes as she played away at the piano that had been her mother's way back in Miles City and had cost a pretty penny to get over here. Whether it was the plumpness or the dresses all printed with wee flowers or perhaps her soft curled hair, which had turned white before she was thirty, Myra seemed to have wandered from her own time. There should have been mandolins.

She usually played about this time in the afternoon. Hilary heard the drift of her long fingers on the keys and, at the proper moment, her light, girlish voice.

Nita . . . Juanita,
Ask thy soul if we must part. . . .

Hilary worried mildly about her mother from time to time because, however sensible the marriage may have been in the first place, it had lately become clear to her that her mother's feeling for her father was excessive. Wouldn't it have been wiser, having survived courtship and rapture, childbirth, measles, mumps, and scarlet fever, to ease off a bit? But no. Clear as chalk on a blackboard—Myra loves Hank.

Now Myra listened attentively to her daughter—she always did—and when the sad small tale was told she said, "Oh, the poor little thing."

However sorry Hilary was for Mr. Barry she did not think of him as poor or little, although come to think of it, he probably was a little under average. But of course her mother had meant Mrs. Barry.

"Hilary," she said, "that little person has had a lot to put up with."

Well, for one thing, her father had been with them for years and years. "And Hilary, her father was quite a cross old man."

And then Mrs. Barry had had her gallbladder and after the little boy was born, the hysterectomy. "Those things cost *money*. And they've been saving up again. Oh, shoot."

Hilary said, "How would you advise?"

"Why, I don't know," her mother said. "I suppose he should try hard to lay low, and then Mr. Gilpin might take it back. Although," she added thoughtfully, "I'll tell you what. We'll just keep our ears open, because sometimes opportunities come up just when you least expect. I think we won't say anything right now to your father. He's been a bit tense lately, or so it seems to me."

"I'll say." Hilary looked with sympathy upon her mother. "What's eating him, anyway?"

"Why honey, your father's an ambitious man."

Hilary was amazed. Never had she thought of her father as ambitious. For what, name of God?

"And it's hard times, you know, Hilary, for ambitious men. With nobody having any money and the government into everything. No, it's not easy."

So, as she burned, her father burned? Wanted a bigger warehouse, more employees, a seat on the City Council, perhaps to be a director of the bank? Why, they might help each other! And though she doubted that she could get him into Harris tweeds or onto the golf course, still in a monied man, much can be overlooked.

But what were they to do with her mother?

Myra never considered anything important except her family and her personal honesty, and no achievement would ever satisfy her more than a three-layer banana cake. For a moment Hilary was so impressed with her mother's simple goodness that she was tempted to drop all her plans and be a good woman, not a better one.

Then their rapport shattered, because Myra said, "But Hilary, I don't see why a grown man like Mr. Barry should discuss such things with a little girl like you." And then she attacked the most beautiful woman in Missoula.

She said, "That mother of Amelia's: she does the same thing, too."

7

AROUND THE GARDEN CITY where the Five Valleys meet—the Missoula, the Hellgate, the Bitterroot, the Mission; the Black-foot—the hills gallop like gargantuan beasts; indeed one of them is named Jumbo; Hilary liked to watch them from her bedroom window when they were saddled with snow and, this time of year, she liked to watch from the roof outside her bedroom window. It was a shallow roof, she could not possibly fall off, and as private a place as you could find in Myra's merry house, a good place to rejoice or plot or to be melancholy. You could take a pillow out there and, stretched upon your back, gaze up at the enormity of the stars as they drifted and circled with the hills.

Also, you could smoke.

On that particular night Hilary had an empty tomato can—at least it was empty of tomatoes; she had a half-inch of water in the can, and two wrinkled Camels, either of which she could quickly douse if that seemed wise. The moon was very bright. It washed the top of Mount Sentinel and winked upon the whitewashed stones of the *M*. Everywhere throughout the West, there is an *M* for Mandan or for the School of Mines or for the University of Montana. They look terrible. For heaven's sake, you do not have to be reminded where you are. Every year the freshmen whitewash the *M*, which is fun for the upperclassmen and for the local children, who watch the long line snaking up with buckets and with brushes.

It isn't a hard climb; when they were little, Doll and Hilary liked to go up there. You took a sandwich and a Milky Way. From the *M* you could spit on the roof of the Main Hall and overlook the green medallion of the Oval, the brown river spanned by its several bridges, and the houses clustered close and then sprinkling out on the far side of town.

Later, there are better and more secret places. Those mountains are ribboned by canyons where a car can pull off and a blanket can be stretched. But while a friend is still enough, Mount Sentinel is a nice place to go. Up there you can think, and on those bald slopes you can see that nobody is sneaking up. However, it was on the bald slopes of Mount Sentinel that Hilary got shot at.

It isn't everyone who gets shot at.

The bullets trilled within three feet of her and the dust kicked up. One came so close that her ankles were showered with dirt.

Of course the woman was not trying to shoot Hilary. But Hilary had made the mistake of letting her brother's impossible dog follow along. The woman was trying to shoot the dog because the dog was running sheep.

It was early spring. A chinook had swept the dry snow from the slope where Hilary stood and had melted the snow below, where the fenced field was shadowed, to a brown sludge. The sheep were dirty, flaps of mud clotted their wool and tails; they were heavy with lambs.

That dog was an Airedale. You used to see a lot of Airedales. As a small pup he had showed some promise; when Myra vacuumed, he rode on the vacuum cleaner. But later, he got interested in sheep. Any dog would. They are silly and they bleat. However, most dogs catch on to the fact that chasing stock is not allowed. Any young person in Montana knows that chasing stock is not allowed. It makes them lose weight and it makes them drop their young. The Airedale was not convinced.

Usually those people complain and then you try to do something about your dog. This woman was not going to take the time. And the trouble was that the dog ran straight for Hilary and the closer he ran, the closer the woman shot. He raced for where every dog thinks a dog is welcome—in a person's lap.

The last bullet whined by Hilary's ear.

She stood up and shouted, "Hey! I'm here!"

Then she stumbled down the mountainside to where the woman stood with the rifle in her hands. Hilary's ankles tottered in her high-laced boots. The woman was quite young, with a voice as dull as her eyes. Her bony wrists were blue.

This woman said, "I didn't go to hurt you."

Hilary said, "But you might have." Her breath was still rough in her throat.

"Yes, I might."

Hilary said, "And then you would have been in trouble."

"I'm in trouble anyway," the young woman said.

So then they parted.

For a number of reasons, Hilary never told. She felt sort of sorry for that woman, who looked so—defeated. Her parents undoubtedly would have made trouble, and some of it for Hilary, who knew very well that she was not supposed to go into the hills alone. Then too, when she saw people shot upon the silver screen it was a pretty special secret to know that in all that audience she probably was the only one—of her age—who had been shot at.

And then a truck hit the Airedale and Hilary thought about the whole thing less and less except on some nights, like this one, when from the front porch roof she looked toward Sentinel and thought, "Right up there. When I was almost shot."

It was getting late. Over on Higgins Avenue the steady stream of cars had lessened and all over her own block the yellow house lights had blinked out and the moon struck the panes with silver. The smell of fresh-cut grass was sweet and heavy. And then behind her the window filled with her father's shoulders, wrapped in a terrible bathrobe that he favored. She dropped the Camel into the can, but the thread of its smoke hung on the dark bright air.

"At it again, I see," her father said, but not unpleasantly.

He swung his leg over the windowsill and his pajama leg slid up. Somehow the red fur on his shanks and calves, which never surprised her when they were swimming in the river, surprised her now. The rest of him followed and he let himself down gingerly on the abrasive shingles.

"I hope you don't throw the butts down on my lawn," he said. "You got another one?"

Considering that the other one she had, she had procured from the pocket of his hunting jacket, she felt she had to share. He lit a kitchen match on his thickened thumbnail with a casual gesture that she much admired. She had burned her own thumb rather badly once, trying to emulate that ease. He drew on the harsh smoke deeply and said, "Aaah." A contented sound.

Then he said, "Your mother thinks you think that I've been cranky." He was astonished. "I suppose once in a while I get cranky. It gets things done. Or stops things from being done. Whichever." He seemed to feel this was a sufficient apology, and because he was a man who never explained anything, perhaps it was sufficient.

Sitting there on the roof in the cold moonlight (it is not warm in the mountains in May, not at night) with their knees pulled underneath their chins, the two of them looked very much alike. This was not unflattering of Hilary. He was harsh-featured, yes, but in his daughter the hooked nose was aquiline and under her plucked brows the eyes lost under the explosion of his brows were big, bright, and clear. By day you could see that their eyes were the same color. Green.

Hank Hunter looked down on his domain and sighed with satisfaction. "This is a good property," he said. "Someday it will be worth a packet, you wait and see. Then you and Dan'll get the good of it."

She didn't want to get the good of it. All she wanted was to be bid Kappa Kappa Gamma and live at the Kappa house and not at home. Anyway, her father's reasonable house on a reasonable street was not what she meant by a good property.

She said, "You know Amelia?"

"Yes," he said. "Your skinny little friend. I'm going to tell you something even your mother doesn't know."

Hilary wasn't sure she wanted to know anything her mother didn't know.

He said, "This house is free and clear. There isn't any mortgage on it." His mouth hardened. He said, "Not yet, anyway."

It hadn't occurred to her that her father's house could have a mortgage on it, so she wasn't much relieved.

She said, "You know Amelia's house?"

Who didn't?

"Well, that's what I call beautiful. Like a palace. All cross-grained paneling, and the swimming pool."

Her father said, "Nobody wants those big houses anymore. If she had to put that house up for sale, whatever she asked she wouldn't get it."

"She's beautiful, too," Hilary said. "Mrs. Lacey. Isn't she beautiful?"

Her father looked at her, surprised. He said, "Well, if you like them like a stork."

Then Hilary was torn between. Much as she disliked to have Anne Lacey called a stork, she was pleased for Myra. If your mother is plump it is comforting to know your father is not attracted to storks.

"And," her father said, "you take your Mr. Barry."

Her mouth tightened just the way his tightened. She had never thought of Mr. Barry as her Mr. Barry, but she saw her father was going to say something critical and she knew she wasn't going to like it. But it turned out the only thing her father was criticizing was Mr. Barry's house.

He said, "Since he got the sack, it's lucky that he rents. You couldn't move that little house this year."

"How did you know?" Hilary demanded.

"Oh, it's all over town."

Hilary said, "I happen to think he's a very nice man."

Hank said, "So do I. Always liked the fellow. I hope he hasn't been giving you ideas."

She knew well enough what kind of ideas he didn't want his daughter given: the unions have some rights. Government is responsible to citizens. Every company town is a police town. Wild Bill Hayward was a saint. Some things the Russians were doing over there were right.

No, Mr. Barry hadn't been giving her ideas.

She said, "I already have my ideas."

"Hmm," he said doubtfully. "His house needs a new roof. From up here, you can see it."

You could see other things from up here, too.

Below, a very expensive car with a Helena license plate slithered by and did not stop in front of Doll's house. Instead, it rounded the corner of the block and stopped there. After a long moment a small shadow slipped from the shadow of the expensive car and into the back alley. The car pulled almost silently away. Nobody who is still in high school is supposed to know anyone who can afford a car like that.

Hilary was wild. She had told Doll and told her. There was nothing that could be done about it tonight but in the morning she would have a thing or two to say. She moved her bottom. The roof had begun to scratch.

Her father shifted, too. "I better get back in," he said, "or she'll be calling."

As if on cue, her mother's soft sweet voice rose from the darkened house.

"Hank? *Oh*, Hank!"

"There she is," he said, pleased. He swung back over the low windowsill and then poked his rusty head out once more. "Just remember," he said, "those shingles aren't asbestos. Anyway, she doesn't like it when you smoke."

8

AND THAT SAME NIGHT.

Across the street, in the cubicle they all conspired to call her bedroom, Doll undressed in the dark, gleefully. The cubicle used to be a dinette, but who needs a dinette? It was just big enough for her bed, a bureau that had been painted white but had yellowed, and a slipper chair covered in a weak cretonne that was the very last thing her mother had sewed for her. There was one window, through which she had entered.

She didn't mind the size of the bedroom, although when her friends came visiting, they had to sit on the bed. She didn't even mind that she didn't have a closet; she kept many things in boxes under the bed and anything that had to be hung was hung in the hall closet. She did mind about the doors. One opened into the kitchen and one into the living room, where there was often someone living.

Her father had the bedroom. Her brother slept in a narrow cot on the glassed sun porch and was bad-tempered. He minded very much not having a closet. He had been sullen ever since his friends went on to the University and his father had finagled a job for him reading meters for Montana Power. He paid his father board. They both expected a great deal of Doll.

Getting out of the house was easy, but there must be some better way of getting in. She was going to put her mind to it.

"Where are you going now?" her father would ask. "What are you up to?"

Doll had learned that the safest thing is to tell part of the truth.

She would say, "We're just going to ride around."

Her father knew the kids rode around and he knew that Hilary's father often let her have his Plymouth to ride around in. He thought Hank Hunter made a big mistake, but it was no skin off his.

"Don't be late," he would say. "Did you get those buttons back on my shirts?"

Tonight that was exactly what she had been doing—riding around. But not with Hilary.

Hilary used to be a lot of fun; not lately. She was always talking about how things looked. Who cares how things look? As long as nothing unpleasant happens as a consequence. And lately, Hilary was always looking ahead and what she looked ahead to seemed to Doll to be a whole lot.

Doll's own wants were simple. She wanted older beaux, because they could afford more. By older, she meant about twenty-two. After that men seem to have other things on their minds. This fellow was twenty-two, he could afford a lot and as far as she could see he had nothing on his mind. What's more, he was an SAE and often sang about it.

> Violets, violets—emblem of fraternity.
> With your perfume memories come
> Of Sigma Alpha Epsilon. . . .

You would think that from Hilary's point of view he would be just the ticket.

Well, he wasn't.

"Do you want to be known all over as a townie?"

What difference did it make? Doll was a townie.

"Has he had you to the House?"

No, but he would.

"Have you met his folks?"

How could she? They lived in Helena.

"Do you double-date?"

Well, there are a lot of reasons why a person wouldn't double-date. For one thing, a person can like another person well enough so that he doesn't especially want to double-date. Besides, what's to do on double-dates? In Missoula? You can't eat all night long. If there are four of you, you can't park. Movies are no fun. It was no wonder everyone wanted to get out to California.

"The fact of the matter is," Hilary said, *"You let him pick you up."*

How else are you going to get to know a fellow?

Unless at school. But the ones at school always seem to have something wrong with them, over and above the age they are. Take this Jon Powers that Hilary thought was such a catch. That is the way he spelled it. Jon. His father was a lawyer; that was supposed to be good. Weekends, Jon caddied for his father's friends and in return, when he got to the University those friends would see that he got bids from the right Houses. But in some ways, Doll thought, he wasn't even a nice boy. He was too pale, his face was narrow as an ax, and he laughed at things you can pretend not to notice unless somebody laughs.

Hilary said that it didn't matter one bit whether or not you liked the person you went out with now. That was all right for Hilary because she had all the time in the world and four whole years to meet the college fellows. Doll had to find a husband P.D.Q. before the fellows that she met were taken.

There wasn't anything wrong with the boy with the black curly hair except that he didn't hang around after school. By and large, the farm boys didn't. They were needed home. And Doll did sort of wish he didn't wear work shoes. Those ones that come up to the ankles? It was the shoes that had made Hilary decide that he was poor. He probably was; many are. Hilary would have rathered Blucher boots but goodness, Blucher boots cost eighteen dollars. Nobody has eighteen dollars.

Anyway, he was too young.

Doll groped under her pillow for her pj's, knotted the top around her little middle, and slipped into her clean bed. This SAE was so going to take her to the House and probably during Track Week, when there were record hops.

Hilary had said flatly, "No he won't."

But he would so. You know what he had said this very night? He said, "You're pretty as a toy."

She reached for the candy box where she kept her bobby pins, and with the help of her white teeth, she opened two of the pins and shaped two curls of her soft springy hair, one at each ear. Then she lay smiling and stroked her small breasts gratefully, because it was fun to be young and pretty as a toy.

Over across Higgins Avenue in the vast bedroom that had been Will's parents' and might as well be yet for any mark that she herself had left upon it, Anne Lacey wandered lightly and restlessly.

It was a room you could wander in. The great bed sat apart in an alcove and there was still room enough for two islands of furniture, one appropriate to the boudoir and one to a sitting room. Anne hadn't turned the lamps on; didn't need to. She had paced that room often enough to know every foot, and anyway, the moon that hung high, thin and white, flooded the room with a light so bright and critical that every time she passed the pier glass she saw the white drift of her new negligee.

She had thought it might help to buy something. She had awakened racked with irritability. People don't realize how painful it is to be irritable. All day she had felt vulnerable—the slightest remark made her tight with rage. And with the rage came the restlessness that made her life intolerable and always had, except just at first when she had married Will.

Whatever Will Lacey had been, she had not found him dull. He was bright-tempered and generous, and very clever at making her feel good. She honestly did not miss him much. When she married she had been curious to see if all that interested her. It did not. But she did like to be admired and Will always made her feel valuable. Also, he had many friends. Now there was no one but schoolgirls and one cross old man.

Her father had been suspicious of Will's happy nature. He felt it was not appropriate to the rich nor to their severe responsibilities. She was afraid her father had been right, or would have been if poor

Will had lived long enough to lose more than he had had time to lose. In the end, he had let Anne down. He had taken her far from her home and her father (she often forgot that her father was dead); he had bought a lot of stocks that had made money then but were not making money now, and he had left her with a half-witted child.

When she thought of that the tears sprang to her great gray eyes and she could feel them on her lashes. She was not going to go East again, with that child to explain, nor was she going to accept the friendship of Missoula, where one woman had had the nerve to say that there had never been anything like that before among the Laceys. How could she say, pray, when nobody had ever heard of the Laceys?

The moon had moved an inch, but the icy light still leached the color from the Persian rug and flicked cynically the china ruffles of the shepherd and shepherdess perpetually bowing to one another on the marble mantel. Oh yes, there was a fireplace, too. Anne drew the curtains, which would fix the moon. Then, sinking to her dressing table while the new negligee billowed about her narrow ankles, she lit the Sèvres lamp the shade of which Mother Lacey had fashioned with her own hands. Mother Lacey had chosen rose silk for the shade. In the deep indentations the silk was still rose; outside it was sun-struck. From its waist depended a taffeta bow as limp and colorless as an old leaf. But the lamp still gave a gentle light.

There was no picture of Will's mother in the room she had long deserted, but there used to be a picture of his grandmother, for whom Will's affection was, Anne thought, exorbitant. For some unfathomable cause, the picture had been taken with an Indian. "They were friends," Will said. Maybe so, but there was no reason to advertise it.

His grandmother, Will gave her to believe, possessed all of the sturdy virtues. She was frugal, brave—she had come all by herself up the Missouri by riverboat to join her husband. She was generous. That Indian had been her friend because she had nursed his wife and infant through the measles. She had started her married life in a sod shanty and had ended in a mansion. Very well. She also had a stern, unhandsome face and wore her thin straight hair raked to her scalp. Once Will infuriated Anne by saying that in some ways, Amelia reminded him of his grandmother.

"She does not!" Anne cried. "Everyone says Amelia looks like me."

After Will died, she had that picture put up attic.

Now, in the rosy light, Anne Lacey leaned to her own picture in the mirror of her dressing table. She was still beautiful.

But not as beautiful.

Her eyes still held their deep glow and her skin its dear flush. But there, right underneath her chin—she stretched her throat to see if it would go away; it didn't—there was a line as faint as if she had traced it with her nail. Some day that moist pink skin would be as desiccated and pleated as the lamp shade.

Across the hall the child cried in her sleep. Anne turned her radio on. The music from a distant dance band muffled the little whimper. That music surged across black, silent miles, over ranges piled like a giant's crumpled carbon papers where the moon glinted on hidden lakes, patches of crusted snow and where in the open it would pick out from time to time, as with a silver pencil, the bright parallels of the railroad tracks. That sweet and taunting music came from the Coast, from the Coconut Grove, from a place of light and warmth where the men did not like their women cute in pants, but dangerous in brocades and furs.

How? How—ever—with that dependent creature?

Now the child cried aloud. Anne turned the radio up. Perhaps Amelia would hear.

She looked long into the eyes of the pretty woman in the mirror. "We're only thirty-five," she told her tenderly.

The moon moved again.

Myra Hunter turned over and hugged Hank.

9

"OH, MY GOODNESS, NO," Myra said. "I don't think your father would like that one bit. No, indeedy. I understand they used to have wild parties there, and I don't for a moment think your Dad would want you anywhere like that." She thought for a moment and then she giggled. "Do you know," she said, "your Dad and I have never been to a wild party?"

Hilary giggled, too. It was not at all hard to picture Hank at a wild party. He'd be a lot of fun. But Myra? Hilary wasn't absolutely sure what went on at wild parties but whatever it was, her mother wouldn't suit.

All the girls wanted to do was to go up to the lake.

Of course they wanted to go all by themselves with no chaperone. If they were all by themselves, what was the need for a chaperone?

Anne Lacey didn't mind.

"Go ahead," she said. "That is, if Mrs. Phelps will stay."

Somebody had to stay with the child.

Usually at this time of year Spud went up to Little Bear himself to take the shutters down, put up the screens and see that birds hadn't nested in the chimney. There were usually mice.

"You aren't going to like it," he told Amelia. "Not if there are mice."

Amelia didn't want him to think he wasn't needed any more to open up the cabin, but that wasn't what he thought. He thought he was well out of it. He had never cared for the lake, got through his chores as fast as he could and headed back. It was lonely up there. There were mountain lions. That early in the season there wasn't anyone at all on the west side and no one on the east shore either except for the folks who ran the store, and they were not particularly friendly, not friendly enough to make it worth a man's time to row all the way over there. The woman didn't like the lake and didn't like to clean the cabins and didn't like the people who, from time to time, rented the cabins. The man didn't like the woman.

On the other hand, Spud didn't want anyone to think he was too old to do that heavy work. For the last year or two he had worried, not about being old, because he wasn't, but about being older. Anne was always talking about cutting down and when she looked at him, Spud thought she had a speculative look. But of course she wouldn't do that.

"Don't forget to bury the swill," Spud said.

Hilary liked to be one of the people who liked the lake and got to go there. Ordinarily she preferred to go after somebody else had removed the mice. But next week was Track Week, and Track Week couldn't do her any good this year and just possibly might do some harm.

Every year during Track Week the town went to pieces. From all over the state, from Two Dot and Rosebud and Twin Bridges and Deer Lodge and such, the high schools sent teams to compete and the fraternities and sororities looked the teams over. Each group was in the uneasy charge of an unhappy teacher who was not allowed to go to pieces, and accompanied by supporters. Those schoolmates came who could raise the train fare or could get the car, and those older folk who were old grads and thought their boy had a chance to win the decathlon or the shot put. For weeks in Dillon and Hamilton and Silver Springs there were cookie sales and the stores donated space for card tables laden with brownies and gingerbread. You couldn't get out of the drugstore without some gingerbread.

The only girls who went—officially—were cheerleaders, but a lot of girls went unofficially and after the fun was over, a lot of reputations did not survive. In the heat of the moment some things were overlooked that would not ordinarily be overlooked, but after the band music died and the snake dance petered out, people started to think again. This is what people do.

Hilary did not intend to be judged nor did she care to have anyone judged with whom she associated. Among those who did not lose their heads were the alumnae. Some important decisions were made after the housemothers locked up, and woe betide the girl who had made herself conspicuous by drink or loud speech or who had stayed at a hotel or—as in one case that Hilary recalled—worn Mary Pickford curls. In the fall, such were not going to be bid.

If you were not going to be bid you might as well leave the state, or at least get out of town until it blows over—ah, but it never does. Somebody always says, "Wasn't she the one who . . . ?" Or, equally dangerous, "Wasn't it her friend?"

Last year it hadn't mattered. This year it was different. Juniors were not asked to the Track Week parties, but they were noticed. Next year the sheep would be divided from the goats. Not that anyone was asked to be a member until after Rush Week in the fall, a time of hysteria and despair which couldn't very well take place until you had matriculated. And not all girls who would attend the University showed up at Track Week; no indeed. There was the problem of where you were going to sleep. The dormitories were open only to the cheerleaders. Careful girls were not seen even in the lobbies of hotels—how were you going to prove you had not been upstairs? What it boiled down to was that you didn't come at all unless you were the daughter of somebody's friend with a bona fide invitation to be sheltered. It had better be a bona fide friend, too.

So it was local girls who got the once-over and were scrutinized. The best would be invited to the dances. This in itself was complicated. To receive several of these invitations was not good; for if the weaker and smaller houses thought they had a chance with you, you were worth less. Ah—! but one or more invitations from the three established what you could expect in the fall, and that in turn established what you could expect for the rest of your life—at least, that portion you spent in Montana, where grown women wear their sorority pins, at least often enough to make everything perfectly clear.

If you did not belong you were called a Barbarian. Ambitious young men were careful not to date you and you would be forced at last to marry an artist or something like that.

Of course Hilary knew this was nonsense; she didn't need Mr. Barry's contemptuous references to tell her that. But facts are facts. She had given up talking to her mother about it, because Myra didn't understand at all.

"Why, Petty," she would say. "If I were you I wouldn't bother my head about all that. Young people do like to have their little clubs. When I was in school we were the Sunshine Girls and for the longest time we all wore yellow ribbons."

Ye gods and little fishes.

So carefully as a general Hilary made her plans, and since the temptations of Track Week were many and the troops not noted for their self-control, she thought it best to get the troops out of town.

Unfortunately Doll was the one who worried her the most, and Doll's father said no. In fact, he said fat chance. He wasn't born yesterday and was sure there would be boys sneaking around up there. There wouldn't be. There wasn't one of the girls so brazen that she would tolerate a boy up there—that kind of word got about fast. Also, there wasn't a boy their own age who would leave Missoula during Track Week, and the older fellows hadn't noticed them yet, except for the one who had noticed Doll.

All Hilary's father said was, "Can Amelia change a tire?"

"No," Hilary said. "But I can. Dan taught me how."

"All right," he said. "Just don't think you're going to take my car."

It seemed natural to him that anyone would want to go to Little Bear Lake. There where the water was so clear and the fish leaped at dawn and the wind in the tamaracks was the only sound, or the snap of a down branch where a deer moved. He had a lot of confidence in his daughter and had himself taught her how to camp. And none of them was made of sugar; they weren't going to melt.

"Do them good," he said.

When the other two mothers called to see where the Hunters stood (nobody ever called Anne Lacey; she did not return anyone's calls) Myra Hunter told each of them, "Why, I believe it will be just fine. Mr. Hunter thinks it will do them good."

She would never understand Hank the longest day she lived.

And then she began worrying for fear the girls would break their legs or get lost in the woods or drown or encounter fierce animals. Then there were fires, and you do have your fiends. Four little girls out in the wilderness all week?

"They won't stick it out all week," Hank said. "Their grub won't last."

That gave her something else to worry about. But maybe it would rain.

10

THEY ALL WORE boots and Levi's and they all had extra socks and sweaters and warm jackets and slickers too, and bathing suits and sneakers, and they had weenies and hamburger and canned beans galore, and cornmeal to cook fish in, in case they should catch any fish, and they had paper cartons filled with fruit and they had two cakes—one chocolate and one not—and plenty of bread and packaged rolls and cigarettes.

They also had a quart of whiskey.

That was Hilary's idea. She didn't feel that any of them was experienced enough to face their senior year without some idea about their capacity. Up until now, it had not been a problem. For the most part they spent their time at one another's houses, where one parent or another usually hovered around. Whether or not the boys felt responsible to the parents, none wished to be eliminated from the gatherings. Of course the boys claimed to have liquor out in the car and did a good deal of coming and going, after which they would guffaw and stagger about a bit, but Hilary had reason to think it was only beer they had out there, if they had anything.

Next year it would be different. Everyone drank at the senior games and dances: always had. Everyone knew the bootlegger who lived up the Rattlesnake in a tawdry attractive cabin and liked kids. Since Repeal, he was lonely, and glad to see the young people and to let them have a jug of gin.

And this summer the fellows would be working, if only for their fathers; that meant that by fall they would have more money. She could see how it was going to shape up. Besides, there was a lot of drinking at the sorority houses and if one were lucky enough to be asked one was going to have to drink. The wise older girls would watch you closely. If you refused you were a drip, but if you couldn't handle it you were a loss. Opportunities for experimentation being limited as they were, it seemed a mistake to pass up this one.

Getting hold of a bottle was not hard; the question was whether, for four, one bottle would be enough. Nobody thought it would be too much, not for four. The way to get hold of it was to snitch it.

Hilary wasn't sure whether her father drank or not, so she assumed he didn't. She wasn't counting the pint he took when he went hunting, or the one her mother kept in the medicine chest: these were precautionary. If by the holidays no one had had pneumonia her mother used the brandy up for puddings and obtained some new. She was a great believer in things being fresh. But if Hilary had tried to snitch liquor from her house, the snitching would have been noticeable.

Kathy's father drank but only right after payday, since that is the only time professors can afford it. It had been hard on him the year the University had to pay salaries in scrip, since not even the friendly bootlegger had been willing to trade liquor for scrip. When he could, he bought a gallon of gin, which the bootlegger, having looked carefully up and down the street, delivered at the back door in a laundry bag.

"I don't usually deliver," he told Kathy's mother. "But for you, the service is free gratis."

Then Kathy's father would place the gin upside down in his closet and let it drain through charcoal. English professors don't usually know about this sort of thing; maybe someone in Science tipped him off. When Kathy first began to go out nights, he told her never, never to drink gin.

"Much of the gin you run into isn't safe," he said.

Because around the first of the month her parents entertained quite a lot, and because as the evening wore along people got careless and left their glasses on the kitchen shelves and even in the bathroom, Kathy knew very well what her capacity was, but she didn't tell Hilary because she wouldn't disappoint Hilary for anything in the world. She liked her.

If Kathy had simply asked her father for some gin he probably would have given it to her, but it wasn't reasonable to ask enough for four. Janet couldn't help because her father and her mother drank only beer. So Amelia took a bottle from her mother's rather large supply. Anne wouldn't notice.

They wanted to leave before dawn, because half the fun lay in abnormal hours and the rest in being away from home: the sooner the better. Myra Hunter would not allow it. *In the dark?* So the mist was rising from the steel surface of the river and the first canyon still purple with shade when they began to rise through the brown hills to the heavy timber high above.

As they settled into the cold car and after they had arranged their purses and their legs, Kathy leaned back and lit the first cigarette of the day. If Kathy had a fault, Hilary had decided, it was that she read more than was necessary and was always quoting from whatever she had read. She said now:

> Journeys end in lovers' meetings,
> Every wise man's son doth know.

"Not this time," Hilary said grimly.

11

MYRA HUNTER HAD planned to worry herself sick, but do you know? The moment the girls turned the corner and were out of sight, she began to enjoy herself. She was almost never up at such an hour, and she felt quite daring standing there in her nightie and looking out at her neighbors who didn't know that she was there. All up and down Hilda Avenue the neighbors slept. Their neat lawns paled to green and in the flower beds the flowers perched, pale moths on their silver stalks. The early air smelled strange. She stood there, sly and daring, until the paper boy's bicycle slid down the street. Then quick as a wink, she scooted back inside.

Upstairs, she tiptoed past her men, both of whom lay abandoned to sleep, their churned covers bunched about their legs. Then in a crisp housedress and in the kitchen, she started to make the coffee with eggshells in it, the way her husband liked it. Their relationship was close but fairly formal; she often thought of him that way: as her husband.

That egg simply flew from her fingers and splattered on the floor.

"Oh, pshaw!" she said.

Eggs are hard to get up from floors. They slide. And then the floor must be washed and of course, you have lost the egg. The incident was disquieting to her because for some odd reason, it had happened several times of late. And she had always been so careful! When the men thumped down smelling of Ivory Soap, Myra had doughnuts frying and more eggs simmering in cream. The Hunters did not think much of cereal.

Myra would not see hide nor hair of Dan all day, nor tonight either, because he was staying over with his friend. There was no reason to worry about the boys. She knew very well what they were going to do and she regretted it, but only mildly, because the rest of the year Dan had good manners and his friend had fairly good manners, too.

But they were going to sneak in free to the track events: it was a point of pride. Naturally Hank would have given his son money for a ticket. You could get tickets at student prices that covered all events: who wanted one? As Dan pointed out, nobody wanted to hear the speech contest nor see the one-act plays. And he supposed you could present your fifty cents and go in through the gate, but if you did everyone was going to know your father had given you fifty cents. What kind of a boy needs fifty cents? No—what you did was sneak in when somebody wasn't looking or, better yet, go up on the flanks of Mount Sentinel, which overlooked the playing field. They couldn't keep you off the mountain. Everyone has the right. Later they would sneak around and spy on parked cars.

Meantime, Myra had the livelong day to herself. She couldn't think when!

After the dishes were done and the fat was cooling, Myra thought of useful things that she could do with a whole day to herself. She could turn out the closets. She could re-pot begonias. She could let down skirts. However, she could do those things any day. So since she wasn't going to worry—Hank said there was a telephone the girls could row to and a ranger station and he said it was ever so much too early for forest fires—what was she going to do with the whole day?

So first she played a few things on the black piano: "Dardanella" and "Sly Cigarette." And then she put "Ramona" on the Orthophonic and danced around a bit, Spanishy. Even then, it was only half-past nine.

So she asked little Mrs. Barry to come for lunch.

Mrs. Barry said it so happened that she could, since Mr. Barry didn't coach any track events and was home and could stay with the little boy.

That made the morning speed. You do not offer a lady the same sized sandwich you would offer a gentleman, and if you are going to use the tea-cloth, no matter how carefully it was put away it must be ironed again to get the creases out, and you must iron it on a Turkish towel, upside down so the embroidery will stand out, and then you have the problem of the Turkish towel and how to make its nap stand out. But these are pleasant problems.

"Why, I don't know when I was last in your house," Mrs. Barry said. "Or you in mine!"

They both allowed.

Now Myra was at a disadvantage because she was sorry for Mrs. Barry and indeed worried for her, and these are things a hostess may not discuss. While Mrs. Barry had much to discuss: none of it comfortable. It was obvious that she was unaware of her husband's problem, but had taken his opinions much to heart. She wished to speak of social crises, of the unemployed, and of the starving children.

What is a hostess to do, poised with whipped cream and pecan pie, when her guest cries, "Oh, their swollen little bellies!"

And then her discourse moved to tramps. Had Mrs. Hunter noticed how well educated they all were these days?

"Frankly," Myra said, "no."

One of the reasons Myra had been glad to live on Hilda Avenue was that the question of tramps did not come up. On the outskirts of town and by the railroad tracks, naturally you got tramps as they came and went, being—as the world knows—men who do not choose to work and who would rather come and go. Her own father, who had been a generous and kindly man, had always referred to the I.W.W. not as the International Workers of the World but as the I Won't Work. Of course that was some time ago and possibly times had changed.

"Unemployed educated men," Mrs. Barry said, suddenly looking frightened. "They put a sign on your house if you've been kind enough to share, and then the next one knows that here is a kind person who will share."

What kind of sign, Myra wondered? Perhaps Greek?

And then they spoke of the President of these United States. Mrs. Barry came right out and asked who Myra had voted for, and Myra thought that a very personal thing to ask. Of course she voted; she voted constantly because it was the American thing to do. She never thought about who to vote for because her husband told her who to vote for, and he voted for whoever he thought best for ice and coal. However should she know who would be best for ice and coal? Across the teapot she looked closely at Mrs. Barry, who did, when you thought of it, have a sort of dark cast to her skin. Myra wondered if she came from some sort of foreign folk. Not that there are not many nice foreign folk, because there are.

Then Mrs. Barry spoke of housing in the Appalachians and of lung disorders in the coal fields and of migrant workers. Myra grew restive. She got up and down quite a lot, making sure each time that her skirt had not caught where it was not supposed to catch.

"I don't know what we're coming to," Mrs. Barry said. "Mr. Barry thinks we may all meet on the barricades."

Just before she left and after she had thanked Myra, she looked at her with her dark eyes that seemed sunk in shade and she said, "Mr. Hunter is lucky to have his own business. He can't be unemployed."

Myra watched Mrs. Barry scuttle across the street and thought indignantly that husbands (if they have nice little boys) ought to knuckle down and not go around saying everything they thought. Then she put a little lavender water on a handkerchief and put the handkerchief on her brow. But in her mind's eye she still saw Mrs. Barry, who come to think of it did look a little Polish, sitting beside a railroad track—probably the Milwaukee— while the little boy shrank, except for his belly, and Mr. Barry went from house to house hoping for handouts.

Myra certainly didn't know what to do about any of it, but then she thought of one thing she could do and she felt better.

She would make no mark on the back door, because Hank wouldn't like it. But she took one of those handy cardboard pieces that keep the layers of Shredded Wheat apart, and on it with an old crayon she had been saving she made a cross, because a cross means the same thing to all people at all times, and she took it out to the back alley because a tramp might feel shy about coming through the back gate, and tacked it to the fence to indicate that she, Myra Hunter, was willing to share.

12

THAT NIGHT AFTER SUPPER Hank Hunter took his wife out to see the town; she looked a little pensive. God knows he had seen all of the town he wanted to see for one day. The damnedest people acted up during Track Week, people who had nothing to do with Track Week or even with the University. One of his drivers hadn't shown at all, and everyone in town wanted extra ice.

But Myra didn't get out much except when Hilary took her shopping, and with the kid out of town for a couple of days (you could be sure it wasn't going to be more than a couple of days) she might like to see the sights.

Her face lit right up. She went upstairs and came back down in a dress that looked just like the other one except it was made of different stuff. At the neck she wore Hilary's Add-a-Pearl necklace with the five good little pearls. He thought she looked very nice but then, if you asked him, she always looked very nice.

They did what everybody did. They drove downtown on Higgins to the Northern Pacific Railroad station and then they drove back up to the University and around the Oval. The traffic was heavy and half the cars were honking, not for any reason but just for the hell of it. On University Avenue, from the big white houses, light flooded over the green lawns and onto the white flannels the boys wore and the bright dresses of the girls.

Myra turned to look over her shoulder. "My," she said, "party dresses are long again. Aren't they pretty!"

Yes, they were. Prettier, if you asked him, than what they wore a few years ago because the truth is that most girls never had the legs for it. Not so pretty was one kid in his flannels hunched on a running board and already throwing up, or the fistfight going on in back of the high school.

Among the sights were the banners strung high over Higgins Avenue and his own son with his friend, hitching a ride on the back of a truck. Yes, he saw Dan and Dan, seeing him, dropped quickly off and vanished into an alley. Hank would have a word with him later on.

Fortunately, Myra hadn't seen. She had been looking the other way and she said now, "Wasn't that little Doll? Why, I believe I saw her with quite an older young man!"

Probably. Nobody seemed to have a lick of sense.

If there was one thing Hank prided himself on, it was a lick of sense. He'd had to, to come from a snot-nosed kid shoveling out somebody else's barn to a man with his own Ice & Coal, and he wasn't through yet. Not by a long shot. You had to have sense and you had to be able to figure out ahead.

Crossing the bridge for the last time they passed the Barrys with their little boy walking hand in hand between them. Probably headed for the picture show, when he ought to be staying home out of sight, figuring out how to keep his mouth shut.

It was too late for the little boy to be up.

The Barrys waved at the Hunters and the Hunters waved back.

If the truth were known, in some ways Hank agreed with Mr. Barry. Everyone knew the big companies had too much muscle. He even agreed about the new President. Hank hadn't voted for him, but next time he probably would. That didn't mean he was going to go all around town saying so.

He had changed his mind right after Inauguration—whew, did the feathers fly! Banks had begun to fail and then people got scared and took their money out of healthy banks and then those banks sickened and went under. Hank had been sweating blood for what he had in his bank (it was a lot more than anybody knew). If he lost that! Then the new man closed all the banks and gave them time to get in order and the people time to get over sweating blood. When they opened up again they almost all opened up.

That meant Hank Hunter could look ahead again.

What he saw ahead was that the Ice & Coal wasn't going to last. Maybe you could keep a two-bit business going, but a two-bit business wasn't what he meant to leave his son.

His own father had lost every cent he had trying to have something to leave his son. He had scrounged and saved all his life and worked for other men and then he went and put it all in a little bitty place over near Shoup, Idaho, where he meant to run sheep. Hank wouldn't have let him, but Hank was overseas. Sheep, his father wrote stubbornly, were just the thing—the Army couldn't get enough of mutton or of wool.

Then the war ended.

And even if there ever was another war, they might not make the uniforms of wool. People were getting rid of their coal furnaces and of their iceboxes and they were getting rid of their land, too, but not because nobody wanted it. Hank, for one, wanted it and already owned more around here than anyone knew except the bank.

People said two things about the Treasure State—that it had the highest consumption of alcohol per capita in the union, and that it was the only state that was losing population. Maybe so. They'd be back. Hank didn't bother with cattle land because the big spreads could afford to tread water. It was the little fellows who were going under and when things got better (things always do get better) the little guys were not going to own the little ranches. Hank couldn't compete with the Mormon Church.

But everybody has to have a place to live, and though some took off, some stayed and had families and went to work for the sugar beet factory or the sawmill. As those people moved into the boardinghouses and frame bungalows over there, others built over here, and who were they going to have to buy the lots from?

You bet your boots.

Myra had been a big help because she never asked for anything and never wanted to know whether they were poor or not as long as she could set a good table and the kids weren't sick. If she ever asked he was going to tell her they were poor, but they weren't. He thought he might have a little trouble with Hilary later on, but so far he had been able to keep the lid on.

He glanced at Myra, who was everything a woman ought to be. She was generous but frugal, so that she could be generous without a bad conscience. He had no idea whether she was brave or not but it didn't much matter because if he could fix it, she'd never have anything to be brave about. Best, she was true blue.

His own mother had shown his father a clean pair of heels when Hank was five, for a fellow who dealt blackjack in a joint in Meaderville. His father never told him that, but a good friend of the family did. Some good friend always tells. Most places won't take on a hand with a kid, but his father wasn't about to leave Hank with any good friend and sooner or later someone would take him on because he was a good worker and would stick.

There were a couple of vacant lots close in and one out on the far side Hank had his eye on. As long as he was wasting time and gas, he might as well have a look-see.

"Mind if I turn off here?" he asked, and turned before she answered. "Why Hank," she'd say. "Whatever you think."

She said, "Why Hank, whatever."

On one of those lots there was a miniature golf course, on one pony rides, and on the one way out a root beer stand. Somebody got excited and said, "See? It don't take no capital to speak of."

The town was blistered with places trying to make sales with stuff that don't take no capital. Ducks and flamingos to stick up in your yard. Cute? Home preserves of wild berries, so you didn't even have to buy the fruit. The signs went up and down and the woman who couldn't sell her jam might do better with something from the garret. *Hey, you remember this?*

The miniature golf course was still tented with strung lights, but only a couple of kids were knocking the balls around. The man with the pony rides had given up. But maybe the root beer stand was doing better. Hank hoped so. He wasn't a man who liked to see folks fail. He'd always wanted to make it up to his Dad for that little place over by Shoup, but his Dad died before Hank could make anything up.

"How'd you go for a root beer?" he asked.

"Why," Myra said, "that would be lovely."

And so it was.

13

ANNE LACEY SPENT a lot of time at her mirror. That was because the woman in there was her best companion—her only companion, really—and more interesting than anyone else she knew. What did she do? Oh, combed her hair this way and that. Put a finger on each side of each eye and pulled the skin tight; she looked younger that way, but even when she took her fingers away she still looked young enough. Oh, there were years and years and years ahead. And what was she to do with them?

Perhaps she ought to do more with her money than she did, summon her lawyers east and west and demand to know why she wasn't making more. But then she would have to listen to their evasions and their explanations. Lawyers are dull, dull, dull.

Or perhaps she ought to do what Will used to do and drive around to the ranches that were now hers. Then she would have to listen to the foremen and she would have to meet their wives. The men would want to take her out to the fields to see the stock. The women would press warm whiskey on her and great gray steaming slabs of her own beef. The conversation would consist of excuses: falling prices, rising costs. Blackleg.

No.

When she leaned forward on her smooth elbows the ruffles fell away from her slim wrists. She spoke to the pretty lady in the glass.

"What's the matter with us?" she asked. Then she confided what was the matter with them.

"We're bored," she said.

Later the child awoke. There was a thin high white eye looking at her. She burrowed under the covers and stayed a long time, but when she came out it was still there.

Cold.

Nobody could lock the door because Spud had taken all the keys away after Amelia had thought the child had locked herself into a burning room. Except for Anne's keys. Anne said she was an old woman and would not give hers up. It didn't matter, because the child would never enter her mother's room. Anyway, it was enough to close the door because the doors opened in, and the child had learned to push through doors but not to pull. However, tonight no one had remembered to close the door at all or, to be fair, perhaps Mrs. Phelps, who was a heavy sleeper, had left it open in case the poor little tyke should wake.

It was safer once she was in the hall because the hall was dark and had sides to it: any place with sides is safer. But there was another place where of all places she would like to be, and that was with her sister. She didn't know Amelia was her sister, but she had small impressions that fitted into a good thing: a gentle voice, a tallness, a warm firm hand. And she knew where that tallness slept and had a long warm back and wasn't cross.

She pushed into Amelia's room. The door swung to behind her. There was no one warm in the bed. Her bitten fingers searched and found nothing but flatness. Then through the window the same cold eye looked at her.

She tried to push back through the door but the door wouldn't push. So for awhile she ran about the room, beating and bumping like a bird in that cold light.

In the morning, Mrs. Phelps got quite a turn. When she found the child she was curled asleep in Amelia's bathtub, which had sides.

14

THEY CERTAINLY WEREN'T city girls, but the fact of the Rocky Mountains didn't make them country girls, either. Two of them had never been on a horse and the two who had, like children anywhere, had been hoisted up and led around. They were accustomed to electricity, running water, and being able to walk to the movies. They had all watched their feet deflected in cold shallow streams, slept under canvas, heard the wind nestle in pine needles, but never without a parent or counselor to shriek at them if they got out of sight. That morning as they drove and as the signs of human life had disappeared, they were quelled by their awe of the mountains, as well as the chill cramp of the small car.

At first there were clutches of small houses huddled beside some old frame store with a gas pump. But after Bonner, where the big logs bumped and the sawdust rose in miniature ranges, there were no gas pumps. Hilary's eyes slid to the gauge. Full.

Naturally Spud was not going to let Amelia take the car out with no gas. Still.

From time to time they passed a dead ranch house. The barn roofs sagged, the fences tottered, air moved critically through cold vacant doorways. No dog barked. A bony horse or two wandered loose and cropped short grass among scattered rock-fall.

Oddly enough these tall and Gothic buildings had been placed under the mountain slopes with the thin morning sun a field away. One supposed the man had voted for the windbreak and the woman had given up the notion of geraniums. In the hard yards broken machinery rusted. Weathervanes swung listlessly. Hilary knew her father would say these people—whoever they had been before they moved away—had used bad judgment. What did they think they could raise in a canyon?

It was good to be higher, where no one had even tried. Hilary hated failure. It made her ill at ease. So did Amelia's driving. Amelia was a rotten driver. Fairly staid within the city limits, she drove now much too fast and with a terrible nonchalance. She rounded curves in a way that made Hilary close her eyes, and passed the occasional car or truck with a sudden burst of speed and a calculated chance that she could get back into her own lane again.

What's more, she drove stylishly, with one gloved hand on the wheel and one casually resting upon the window frame as if to show that driving a car meant nothing at all to her. Hilary felt that her thoughts were far, far away.

Janet and Kathy, giggling in the back seat, didn't seem to notice. The professor could not afford a car and the doctor did not permit his daughter to drive his. The nondriver accords a blind confidence to the experienced, does not seem to query the value or type of the experience. By the time that they reached the high open country, Hilary found that her nails had left faint stigmata on her palms. Hilary said casually that she would spell Amelia if she wished.

"I'm fresh as a daisy," Amelia said.

Presently, having run out of chatter and not being ready for philosophy, they sang. All healthy young sing of despair and disaster. They implored the willow tree to conceal them, they affirmed a simple confidence that their men would stop beating them. They had the blues.

And then, as westerners will, they turned sentimental about the West. They sang of Little Joe the Wrangler, who got his in a stampede.

> He was riding Old Blue Rocket with a slicker,
> o'er his head. . . .

It was not clear whether the boy or the horse wore the slicker, but of course if it were the horse it explained a good deal.

> . . . and beneath the horse, mashed to a pulp—
> his spur had rung his knell. . . .

"Jupiter!" Kathy said. "My father will love that!" Just then a small thing happened that they found unsettling. For some time they had been aware that there was, far in the road ahead, a dark speck against the white dust of the road. It grew larger. It was the devout wish of each of them that it would be four-legged. But they knew that it was not four-legged.

A man in himself is not alarming unless he demonstrates some malice. What disturbed the girls and kept them silent (it seemed safer not to mention it) was that a man on foot was incongruous up there; the incongruous is frightening. Then, too, if his horse had got away or his car broken down, it was incumbent on them to offer help. Immediately there was set up in each of them unpleasant conflict. No one in the West passes up anyone in trouble. Only Californians do that.

However, in the last few years a great many desperate men wandered the roads with no homes, no work, and no prospects, and some of them were armed. Even in better times young women are not to pick any stranger up. John Dillinger was still at large.

They did not really truly think they might be raped or shot, but they did really truly think the man might take the car and leave them stranded on the road. Now who was best equipped for that, four girls or a grown man, possibly armed?

Hilary had a mean, true thought. She was glad she was not driving, and she was glad that it was not her father's car. Assuming that the girls themselves were safe, her father would be wild if anybody took his car.

Amelia stepped deeply on the gas and they went by.

Worn clothing, bowed shoulders, and a ravaged face. None of them looked back for fear he should be standing there looking after them, perhaps with one soiled, horny hand still raised in supplication.

But the glad mood of the morning was gone.

"Anyway," Kathy said, "he wasn't young, but he wasn't old either. Not really old."

That made them all feel better. The young are strong and capable, and a young man, later on, might very well look back on such an experience as adventure. Nobody wishes to insult the old. They were glad Kathy had taken a good look.

She said, "Just about the right age for Dillinger."

A lot of people sort of liked Dillinger, whose exploits and those of his gang enlivened the morning papers. It was not one of those big gangs that were, Spud said, a disgrace to the nation. Dillinger's gang was made up of just a few close friends. And you had to stingily admire fellows who would not be caught, with every hand against them. Well, Dillinger was caught, but say! He broke jail in Crown Point, Indiana, with a carved wooden gun! Hank Hunter said you had to admit.

However, a small gang (when you know where it is) is one thing, and a lone man at large another. John Dillinger was said to be somewhere in the Midwest, but the F.B.I. don't know everything. A lot of people thought Missoula would be a dandy place to hide out, and as a matter of fact Janet's mother had a friend who lived in the Wilma Building and had seen him there. She was on her way to the elevator when in the next apartment a man's face looked through the transom! No one looks through transoms. Why would they? And you would have to get a chair and all like that. So it was probably Dillinger, which she reported to her friends, though not to the police. The Wilma Building seemed a reasonable place to hole up. The Wilma Theatre was right downstairs and after dark you could sneak down and see the current attraction. Little Bear Lake did not seem so reasonable.

"Except," Janet said (she was the authority because it was her mother's friend), "there are those boarded-up cottages where anyone could hide."

They were silent, thinking of the boarded-up cottages for which they were headed.

Hilary said, "But what about supplies?"

Here they came with supplies.

Each of them felt a small frisson of fear. "Nonsense," Hilary said. "They wouldn't have let us come if there were any chance."

What people who owned at Little Bear liked about what they owned was solitude. You couldn't see the cabins from the dirt lane that snaked the shore. On either side the tamaracks were tall. From the lane the land fell steeply to scattered clearings; some people had put in wooden steps and some plain scrambled. In either case much had to be lugged and many a sprained ankle was sustained, particularly if there had been merrymaking.

Even from the water, though you might see sun glint on a screened porch, the cabins were not easy to identify unless you belonged, in which case you recognized docks and boathouses. No cabin was named, nor did any sign proclaim its owner. This was the result of the same agreement that forbade running water. You had an outhouse and a shallow well with a hand pump. You washed outside if you felt you must wash. Half the fun was pretending to be your own ancestor.

It was a grievous disappointment, then, when the Grovers opened Groveland. Get it? The one owner over on that side put his place up for sale and the Grovers bought it and moved in even before the low frame store was completed, the dance-hall or the one-room cabins. Everyone said they would fail. Had to. Little Bear did not attract that kind of person.

Well, now it did. Motorboats shattered the silence that, before, had been broken only by the rattle of glacial streams and on a clear Saturday night you could hear the distant sound of jazz. For on Saturday nights all kinds of persons came out of the woods to drink and fight and gamble—not only the wrong kind of person up from town but ranch-hands from small scattered ranches. Once in awhile a drifter, too.

Like this one fellow who had drifted in this spring, he didn't say from where, and wanted work. Well, they could use him opening up, and Mrs. Grover, who liked the raw tall types and didn't much mind insolence, came out and said so.

Her husband said, "I know his sort. He won't stick."

"Who cares?" Mrs. Grover said.

Before this fellow—his name was Earl—had been there a week she had changed her mind. If he had cut out she would have cared a whole lot. She didn't, herself, find him attractive: there was something wrong about his head. But the girls who worked in the kitchen did. He took them into the woods and out on the lake at night and the sudden coolness between them gave her something to think about.

Besides, she liked his nerve. He'd ask the damnedest things just as if he had a right to know. Who around here had any money? How much? Was that *so!* Sometimes she'd tell him and sometimes she wouldn't. Mostly she did because she liked to talk as well as the next and it was one hell of a time since Joe Grover'd listened to her.

When did those rich people start coming up?

What were those keys?

She was proud of the keys, which hung on a pegboard behind the counter and under the sign that said No Indians Served Here. The keys were a project of her own aimed at those snooty folks across the lake. She sold them the idea that their property would be a lot safer if she had duplicate keys in case of—well, say, fire. She also sold them beer, Log Cabin syrup, and cold cuts.

Not all of them were persuaded but some were. Brundage, Wilson (both J.T. and R.W.), Appleton, Moriarty. Lacey.

"Give me the loan of them," Earl said.

She would not! He was just curious? Well, he could hold his water. Talk about brass!

So that was Groveland, and none of the young people from over here were to go over there. They might be taken for the wrong sort of young people.

They were all hot and snappish by the time they reached Little Bear and they all (except Amelia) felt that before they hauled supplies it would be nifty to have a swim. Amelia said that was not the way it was done. Since she was the hostess, that ended that.

Though Hilary did ask, "Why?"

"It just isn't smart to leave all that around. What would we do without it?"

"But what could happen to it?"

"Someone might take it."

Who, pray? They hadn't passed a living soul except for that one man who, thank God, had not been headed this way.

"Well, then, bears."

That was different. Everyone knew there were grizzlies in Glacier National Park and there were black bears everywhere. They had all heard about the black bear over at Yellowstone who was trapped in an outside toilet. A harried mother with a whimpering child had opened the door and pushed the child inside.

Their eyes slid from the timber to the bushes. Then they began to haul, only hoping that Amelia (who was more bossy here than she was in town) would not insist on taking shutters down and opening up before they had a swim. Maybe a bite, too.

She didn't.

Because someone else already had opened up.

When she turned the key in the lock, the door didn't open. It was as natural and baffling as a dream. She turned it again and this time it opened. Not easily—it never opened easily—but it squeaked and opened. So someone else had left the door unlocked. She pulled it wide. Beyond, where there ought to be a dank dark cavern, the long room was flooded with sun and sweet with lake air. The screens were up, the old ash had been shaken from the stove, the woodbox was filled and the bark swept up.

Amelia should have been pleased, but she wasn't. The others were.

"God bless him," Janet said.

They thought Spud had arranged it for a nice surprise. Amelia knew it was the last thing he would arrange, hoping as he did that the whole trip would be a foul disaster. The pump was primed, the rowboat bumped at the dock. Amelia was robbed of responsibility. There was even fresh toilet paper in the outhouse.

As far as she could see, he who had robbed her had not taken anything. The guns hung on the wall. In the closet, the fishing tackle was undisturbed. She opened a drawer and her father's heavy blunt Smith & Wesson lay deadly in its chamois wrap. In all the years the cabin never had been broken into, but it was damn foolishness to leave valuables about, and she was going to speak to Anne about the guns.

Nothing seemed to be gone from the cupboard shelves, but then, there was nothing to be gone. They didn't leave canned goods behind because cans freeze and burst; no one had forgotten the time that happened. They didn't leave flour or anything in paper boxes because of mice, but they had left paper napkins that the mice had tattered to frowsy lace, and whoever had swept the floor had not disposed of the wee black buckshot on the shelves.

Amelia had thought there was more linen than that, but one sheet is very much like another; how is one to tell? There were blankets and towels and dish towels and a small pile of checkered tablecloths for the big wooden table where on rainy days they played interminable games of solitaire. The bedding would all have to be aired.

On the porch and in the living room there were couches or rather, cots that doubled for couches. During the winter the skinny mattresses from the porch were piled inside so that the snow that drifted through the screening and rusted the bare springs would not mildew them. The one bedroom was her mother's. In there the shutters were down, but so were the old green window shades, so cracked that the sun, striking them, drew maps on their dry lengths. Amelia snapped the shades up and stood considering. Something was wrong in here.

It was not a room that Amelia liked. Apparently her mother had never much liked it, either, for there were few signs of her occupancy. One corner had been curtained off with cretonne. There was a wooden rod back there from which wire hangers trembled, and a low shelf that held her mother's narrow shoes. Amelia lifted the curtain, which was stiff with dust. Nothing had changed in there.

In one corner there was an old iron crib where the child had slept for a summer or two. After that, it had not worked out. The child had liked to sit in the warm shallows and beat the bright water with the small flats of her hands. But she had to be watched every minute. She could fade into the timber before you could turn around. And suppose she drowned. How would that look?

Over the crib, cracked and bleached by the summer suns, was a picture Amelia had tacked there long ago. The Dinkey Bird was singing in the Amfalula tree. The winds of winter, sweeping beneath the cabin, had lifted and wrinkled the thin old rugs. All this was usual. Then what was wrong?

The bureau top was bare; the sun-struck mirror leaning crazily above it reflected only dust. Her mother's celluloid brush and comb (there was no sense in bringing silver way up here) would have been swept into a drawer to brittle in the cold. On the small wobbly table beside her mother's bed, one thing had been overlooked—a book that her mother had tried to read lay open still at the limp pages where she had given up. *Black Oxen*, it was called.

Upon the open pages there were scattered crumbs of Bull Durham.

Amelia drew her breath sharply and with it came a scent that was not her mother's, the kind of cheap dime-store scent that made sitting beside some girls at school unpleasant. They were invariably girls who wore their hair too long and too curly and who used thick lipstick and wet it with their tongues. When they played volleyball their mascara ran. One of them fainted every month wherever she happened to be, which was embarrassing because there was a kind of boy who always laughed.

She yanked the bedspread from the bare mattress and the lumpy pillows, and with distaste she held one of the pillows to her face. Yes. That pillow, too, would have to be baked in the sun. It did explain what had happened to the sheets.

She was not going to tell the others because she knew the others: as soon as the sun went down they would see men behind every tree and refuse to go to the outhouse unaccompanied. She herself was not frightened. It was not the sort of thing that was frightening.

But she shook with rage, because of the purpose to which her mother's room had been put. And she would not bake the pillow. She would burn it.

15

JUST ABOUT THAT same time, Doll got lonesome. All morning she had been too busy to be lonesome. A lot of things had to be done and she was sort of glad to get at them, like taking curtains down and washing off the pantry shelves. Her brother wanted his shirts ironed, which was reasonable. Men can't iron.

But there is something about ironing that doesn't use the whole of you enough. You stand still while your hand moves back and forth, and you get to thinking about some things you'd just as soon not think about. Hilary was right. That SAE had not asked Doll to the dance. He had explained, uneasily, that the brothers had asked him to take a girl from Three Forks because the Delta Gammas were interested in her. The SAE's and the Delta Gammas were very close. He said he would call her right after Track Week: Doll didn't think he would.

Heigh-ho. There went the early marriage and the home in Helena.

It seemed odd, too, to have her friends out of town without her. Why, day after day they brought their lunches to her house, pressed their skirts on her ironing board and left their Coke bottles in her sink. She had a hunch that this was only the first of what was going to happen many times. Usually the phone rang all the time. This morning it had only rung the once.

But one thing Doll had learned. If you like to feel sorry for yourself, you can always find a reason. She'd seen the same thing happen to many others, like her own brother. You are friends all through high school, but then they go on and you don't. At first they try to see you once in a while, but they change and you change, and they get to know people you aren't ever going to know. After a while it's as if you never had been friends.

You just have to make a bunch of brand new friends, and one of them she had already made. His name was Duke. She had been out with him a couple of times and she was going out with him tonight. Duke was pretty old to still be at Missoula High, but everybody can't be smart. Lots of nice guys aren't smart, but mostly they do get a job, some sort of job, and then a little place of their own and pretty soon, a wife.

There are worse things.

Her brother dropped by for a peanut butter sandwich. Doll would have liked a lot to like him, but Aaron was a hard one to like because he felt cheated by everything and wanted to make it plain that that is what he felt.

Doll told him, "Some girl called."

"Yeah?"

"I got her number here somewhere."

"Well, gimme." And then he noticed his shirts hanging in a row. "Hey, thanks," he said. "You remember starch?"

She didn't mind doing up his shirts but she did wish he would remember that she knew the way he liked them done. Of course, by all rights, his mother should still be doing up his shirts. It would be disloyal of Aaron to think his sister just as good with shirts. They both remembered her so well. Her mother had been a gentle woman.

Her father was a cross man, but though she did everything she could to keep him in the dark, she was sorry for him. He didn't seem to have much fun. But she did wish that if her brother patterned after either he had not chosen his father to pattern after, because not in a million years could he be as mean as their Dad was. You can put up with a real mean man; one who is trying to be mean is meaner, maybe because the one who's naturally mean doesn't have to try so hard.

Besides, her father wasn't always mean. She remembered once when he said he was sorry that Doll had to take on so much so early, and then he said, "But look at it this way—some lucky fellow's going to get a dandy wife."

Gratefully she had said, "Oh, *Dad!*"

So far, however, he had done pretty well at keeping all the lucky fellows away.

He watched her just as closely as if his own virginity were at stake. Or thought he did. Fortunately, he was not an observant man. He trusted Hilary Hunter as much as he trusted anyone, because she came from sober folks and lived across the street. He didn't seem to notice that she was no longer ten years old or that the kids they hung around with were no longer girls. Sometimes Doll felt bad to be fooling him and sometimes she felt plain lucky that he was the kind of man who, after supper, either nodded off or went across town to see his lady-friend who lived over there in the Thornton Apartments (Doll and Aaron were not supposed to know). Either way, he moved early into the bedroom and collapsed.

After Aaron left, the house was very quiet. Doll was a person who liked a little noise. The alarm clocks ticked—each of them had an alarm clock to alarm them—and the water dripped in the sink. Unless she remembered that the faucet needed a new washer, that drip was going to leave a urine-colored stain, and then her father would be mad. She turned on KGVO because it was time for the request hour. Somebody asked for "Goofus." Someone older wanted "Casey Jones." Well, "Casey Jones" was kind of catchy.

> Casey said just before he died
> There were two more roads that he wanted to ride.

She hummed along for a bit.

> The fireman said what can they be?
> It's the Southern Pacific and the Santa Fé.

Her interest lapsed. She decided to go across and see Myra and maybe borrow Hilary's new blouse that Hilary honest to God was too pale to wear, whereas the last time Doll had worn it, Mr. Hunter said she was pink as a peony The Hunters were comfortable people.

It just so happened that Myra was frosting a three-layer cake. Brown, white, pink. It was Hank's favorite and Dan liked it too. But she was bored with the cake and about to frost it with a plain boiled white, which would disappoint the men but save a lot of time. Having some company made all the difference, and Doll might like to stir the color in.

Myra was worried about Doll. Not very, because Doll was a good girl, but her mother had been a dear friend and Myra felt responsible. It had been so easy when the little girls were busy with their jump-ropes and their jacks and tea sets. Then all that Myra had to do was to put Merthiolate on their knees and watch Doll's neck and behind her ears. Later they had to be told about strangers and gifts of candy, and there was that one time when coming home after dancing school the girls had seen a man expose himself. Myra had found that difficult to explain because she couldn't see the sense in it herself.

When the boys started coming around there were things she really had to tell them. She waited to tell them both together so that she would not have to do it twice. One afternoon they were in the living room playing the Orthophonic—one record over and over until she thought she'd go out of her mind. They were trying to learn the words, one line of which sounded very much like

Komo-mahi-nokaua-ikka—hallikahela-kaua

which made no sense. From another, too, she could get no real, clear picture.

Where the huma-huma-nupa-nupa-apawaha goes
swimming by!

They would double up and put the dratted thing on again.

Myra spoke up. She said, "Now girls, that'll be enough. Mr. Hunter will be here any minute and he won't like that tune and anyway, there's something I must say before he gets here."

They were all ears.

Myra hated to say what she had to say, not because it was awful because it wasn't, but it did mean they were not little girls anymore. Pretty soon they'd be thinking of homes and husbands of their own.

She explained that they must never meet a boy downtown either by arrangement or accident (knowing as she did that most accidents are arranged). The boys must come to their homes, and they were not to honk at the curb either, but to come right up and ring properly at the door. Also they were not to eat on the street anymore, not so much as an ice cream cone, and they were never, *never* to lean against a building anywhere. Otherwise . . .

"Otherwise," Hilary said, "they'll think we have round heels."

"Oh, my word, Hilary!" she said. "Wherever did you pick up such a phrase?" But then she had to laugh, because it was precisely what she meant.

Myra did not think that the first wave of loutish boys were dangerous except perhaps to her china, as they shoved and guffawed around her living room. They had just not grown into themselves yet. But one of these days one of them was going to run into a young man who had grown into himself.

Hilary would say, "Oh, *mother!*" But Hilary would understand what she meant.

A word to the wise should be sufficient. But Doll, innocently, led her off in a troubling direction.

Because when Myra said, "I expect you miss the other girls, but Doll, I'll bet it's not all that much fun up there," Doll said, "Yes, I miss them. I might just as well get used to it, I guess."

Myra had started at the bottom with the chocolate; it made the cake look more stable. She paused with her knife poised in her hand. Then, thoughtfully, she licked it.

She said, "Why honey, why would you say such a thing as that? When you and Hilary have been best little friends for years and years?"

Doll was matter of fact. "Oh, Mrs. Hunter," she said, "look at Aaron. Aaron and Chuck and Harold used to be best friends, but he never sees them since they went on to the U."

Myra had a wild sudden feeling that the Hunters themselves should send Doll on to the U, though she knew it was impossible, with Hilary ready and Dan coming right along, not to mention Hank's business being bad. And Doll's father would expect her to go right to work, and perhaps really needed the extra. Even in better times, many parents feel they don't owe the children anything once they have graduated High.

Doll said, "It isn't just the money. I'm not smart." She laughed lightly. "Goodness, I never would have got through if Hilary hadn't helped."

Myra thought of the brown head and the copper bent over books in the dining room.

"Just the same," she said, "Hilary's not going to forget her dearest friend."

"No," Doll said. "Sure she won't. But we won't see so much of each other from now on."

Oh, it was wrong. It was all wrong.

So when Doll said, "Mrs. Hunter, is Hilary's blouse clean— the new one? Because I sort of planned to wear it," Myra did not ask where she planned to wear it. Instead she said hastily, "Of course, dear. You go right up and get it. Maybe you'd like to take the Add-a-Pearl?"

But when Doll had retreated with her spoils, Myra finished up the cake moodily. There was a lot going on that she didn't like, not one bit. Her dear friend was gone and her dear friend's daughter was too grown-up for her years—oh, much too much! Next winter those nice Barrys might not have a roof over their heads. When she washed up the dishes after lunch, she had smashed one of her mother's Sèvres cups.

And Hilary, who would not even be eighteen until the Christmas season, was off in the wilderness—not with her own competent father but with three new dearest friends, not one of whom Myra had known as a little one with skinned knees; not one of them from the dear days beyond recall.

16

AMELIA WAS RIGHT. As soon as the sun dipped behind the mountains and long shadows spilled into the lake, the girls got anxious. Even Hilary's confidence leaked with the light. The hard fact was that they were civilized young women who quailed before the out-of-doors, not for fear there should be someone out there, but because there wasn't. Only miles of trees with nothing in them but birds and animals. It wasn't natural. They missed their neighbors. Mind you, you don't have to like your neighbors in order to miss them. You may not have spoken to him since that last thing about the dog, and of course she is impossible. Nevertheless, if they see flames mounting from your roof they will call the fire department, and if your telephone is out of order, you may use theirs.

Of the four, only Amelia had never known a neighbor. Amelia's mother found the thought of neighbors disagreeable and Spud didn't seem to miss them. Yet as the last light left the tall skies and the mountains took a giant step, even Amelia was glad to see, presently, the blue bloom of arc lights across at Groveland.

"Do you suppose," Janet said wistfully, "that from over there they can see our light?"

"I shouldn't think so," Kathy said. It made her feel insubstantial to think of all that light and merriment and music over there where the real world was going on, while here they were suspended in darkness and in silence. "Not unless someone stood right on the shore and watched."

Amelia changed the subject.

They modified their evening plans. The moonlit dip was first to go. After the thin moon rose the shadows blackened; anything could lurk behind that bush. And anyway, the water was too cold. They might drown. Then went their wish to sleep on the screened porch. Screens are no protection. Clawed animals might get in, drawn by the smell of food and perhaps by the smell of girls. There were two cots in the living room and a third girl willing to sleep on the floor.

But Amelia was going to sleep alone and on the porch.

Well, that was up to her.

By the time they had completed an armed expedition out-of-doors with flashlights and an ax, Amelia decided that Hilary was the worst of the lot and, what's more, liked it. Hilary had heard that mountain lions dropped from trees on people. She understood that bears broke right through windows and she suggested candles burning in each window as a deterrent to bears. Amelia vetoed candles, with the purpose of deterring fires. It was decided that they should keep pans beside their beds to bang together in case of bears.

And Hilary determined that it was no time to try the whiskey, since they might need their wits about them and had better be at the peak of their powers.

It was also Hilary who first fell sound asleep.

Kathy tried for awhile to keep things going, but when she intoned,

> By the pricking of my thumbs
> Something wicked this way comes. . . .

she elicited only the feeblest of shrieks. Presently they slept.

Except Amelia. Amelia got up quietly, took the bottle and went down to the shore.

Coming to Little Bear had been a mistake. Back in town, the girls made her feel like a girl: lighthearted, a bit foolish, enviable because of her years and her future. Why, she was never going to die! Up here, they seemed shallow. Their empty chatter, their little plots, Hilary's fake fears bored her. They were just spending time until real life began.

The first drink tasted awful. She had often tasted drinks before, when from time to time she took one to her mother. Tall drinks are safer, because if any amount of a short drink is gone, the recipient is going to notice. Amelia would sip as she walked, which is not easy. Try it. She had never had enough to see what her father saw in it. More and more she felt like the father who had not been able to make his child safe nor his wife happy.

It was nice here in the dark, with the flat clean smell of fresh water. And good to be alone. In the big dark old house in town the doors were always shut, but that did not mean one was alone. Amelia always listened, there, for a sigh or a sob. All day in the crowded, noisy little car, she had heard her mother's sighs. Now they were gone.

The second swallow was easier and with the third, she hardly gagged at all. She wondered if that is why her father had driven so far and fast in the big car: to be alone. Amelia hadn't realized what a peaceful thing it is. To be alone.

She had pulled a rough jacket over her pajamas and had brought a blanket. Wrapped in it and leaning against a boulder she was invisible. But she saw all things. She saw the far side of the lake over the sheets of beaten silver. Over there the narrow shore streaked the darkness, and behind, tamaracks fringed the rising land. It was very late. From the peaks, snow flashed like a semaphore. There was no light anywhere except moonlight and snowshine.

It was hard, being the only one left to look after them. Spud said that was a whole lot of—spit. He said she was too young to look after anyone and that anyway he was left, but he was only an old man who worked for them and pretty soon she was not going to be too young.

The wind moved in the needled branches; ripples spoke quietly on the shore. At her feet mica glinted in the rocks. Back of those peaks there were other peaks and ranges where nothing grazed but deer and elk. She reached for the bottle. Was it all right? It was all right. She scooped pebbles around it so that it stood securely.

Then she giggled.

Once late at night when they were frightening one another, Hilary had asked, "What is the worst sound you could ever hear?" And then she answered. "You are the last person alive on earth. And the doorbell rings."

So when Amelia went back up to the cabin, and she was going to do that pretty soon, because the little moon had moved a long way across the sky (but first she was going to have one more drink of the whiskey), she would wake them by beating at the door. They'd get over it. They had to.

Something went wrong. The moon shrugged behind a shawl of cloud and her mood changed. Why had her father left her? If he had died in the war or from disease or even had been murdered, then he could not have been held accountable. But he had chosen to drink and to drive too fast; he had conspired with his own death and had left Amelia to fill his shoes.

Very well, she would fill his shoes.

The time was late, the air cold, the moon seemed disinclined. Then in the last moment of her solitude a sound came, a small sound, indistinguishable at first from the lap of water, but rhythmic. Dip, drip. Dip.

Oars.

Trouble. A doorbell in the night.

She stood, a bit unsteadily. It could be later than she thought. If it were anywhere near dawn, it might well be a fisherman. In that case, the boat would slip right by her cove. But the boat did not slip by. It slid, a little darker than the water, for the shore. It might be a woman, fishing. Some women like to fish.

But it was not a woman.

The boat nudged the shore, the figure whose shoulders were not womanly shipped the oars. Whoever he was, he had a flashlight that swept the cove with hard yellow light. The light struck her face. His voice was deep and amused, which was small comfort; the mad and dangerous are easily amused.

He said, "What've we got here?"

Then he turned the flashlight on himself and said, "Don't be frightened."

He was big and not very young. He wore his hair in a pompadour that did not hide the fact that his head was slightly flattened, like a horned toad. Or a snake. There was something nasty about him and she was not imagining it, because this was the one. There wouldn't be two, not at Little Bear, not at one time. But she wasn't frightened, she was furious.

This was the one who had soiled her mother's bed.

He said, "I heard there was going to be a pretty lady here. No offense—I meant your mother."

That such a one should mention her mother. That such a person should even be aware of Anne Lacey!

This person said, "I opened up for you. If nobody had come, I wouldn't want to leave your place opened up."

It almost sounded reasonable. But not at this hour of the night. It is hard to command, dressed in an old gray blanket. The treacherous moon flipped the scarf of cloud. Amelia saw that he was quite a handsome man, but not in a nice way. Although it might have been the sick light of the moon that drained his eyes.

She gripped the blanket with one hand. She said, "I will take the key."

She saw him laugh. "I guess not," he said.

Nothing makes you so helpless as a larger person who says he guesses not.

He said, "I'll take it to your mother."

It was hard to be sure in that bad light, but Amelia thought those eyes appraised her and then flicked away as if they found her of no earthly purpose.

He said, "See you around."

She wished to make the child's retort: not if I see you first. Instead, she turned her back on him.

"Here," he said. "You forgot something."

Grinning, he held the bottle out to her.

If she had happened to have her father's Smith & Wesson, she might very well have shot him. And in the long run, it would not have been a bad idea.

17

IF NONE OF IT WORKED out the way Hilary had hoped, it wasn't turning out the way Doll had hoped, either.

When dark seeped into the Missoula Valley and the horns began to blow, Doll left the house quietly. During Track Week her father took for granted she would be with the girls. After her bath her hair curled softly around her face. Hilary's blouse looked pretty good and so did Kathy's skirt.

Thank God she had not borrowed the Add-a-Pearl. You can repair a ripped seam, but there is almost nothing you can do for good damaged pearls.

Just on the chance her father might be watching, she crossed the street casually swinging her handbag. If Myra Hunter wondered why she was headed for the Hunters' alley, she would have to think of a reason fast.

But Doll could always think of a reason fast.

Nobody looked. After the alley she hurried because it was scary there, but it would not be scary where she was going to meet him. Corner of Higgins and Conway.

She had met Duke first at the drugstore where he worked Saturdays and where she bought her cigarettes. He had lifted his lashes (long for a fellow); she had dropped hers. Where was the harm? She had gone out with him a time or two and it had been all right, so when he asked her out again tonight of course she had said yes. It was a lot more fun than sitting around some dumb old lake.

His car was loitering at Higgins and Conway and she was off the curb and into the front seat in a jiff. It wasn't much of a car and it smelled faintly of old throw-up, but it was Duke's own car and not his Dad's.

He said, "You're looking great, kiddo."

In the back seat, somebody snickered. She had not thought that anyone would be in the back seat. Duke stretched his arm behind her and turned his hard profile toward the back, although he kept his sleepy eyes on Doll. His hands were hairy. Oh, he could be in motion pictures, although Doll wished he wouldn't wet his yellow hair like that, so you could see the little paths the comb had made.

He said, "My buddy? Augie. With him, it's Marge."

Sure she knew Augie. Everyone who knew Duke knew Augie. Neither of them went out for track. Augie would have been good at the shot put. He had the shoulders for it, but like a toad (he really did look like a toad), from the shoulders down he dwindled. He had a heavy beard. A book salesman had once taken him for the janitor. Doll had not ever expected to double-date with Augie.

Hilary would say, "Well, what did you expect?" But until now, when Doll went out with him they had been alone.

Marge was built much like Augie but was blonde as Duke, except close to the scalp. She had not finished High and made no bones about it. When she was still going High she was the kind of girl who scuttled into classrooms and sat silent and sulky until the bell and then was boisterous in the halls. Doll remembered that Marge had hated gym because of the showers. She must have crouched well out of the water's way, because when she came out of the shower stall each golden hair was stiff with its original intricacy.

Marge also had a reputation that Doll thought was probably unfair, because how in the world could anybody know? But in the girls' locker room they said, "Well, she goes around with Augie Spenelli, doesn't she?"

"Sure I know Marge and Augie," Doll said. "Hi."

A mouth drawn heavily in purple does not look all that good on a short girl, nor does a low and breasty dress. Marge thought long earrings would be keen. Doll had rather hoped that they would go somewhere where she could see and be seen; one of the beer parlors maybe, although there was a risk of running into Aaron, or even to the Red Rooster outside town, where the older crowd went and were served real drinks. She didn't want to see anything enough to be seen with a breasty dress. No, thanks.

What made her mad was that she had honestly believed she was not stuck up. If anyone was stuck up, it was Hilary. Hilary said she simply used her common sense. She said that in the larger cities you might get away with that sort of thing (Doll wanted to know what she meant by that sort of thing) but in Missoula everyone knew who you ran around with. They would say "Birds of a feather."

But here she was, Doll, feeling the same way. It was probably unfair—Marge was probably good to her mother and faithful to her friends, but there you were. Doll did not wish to be seen with anyone who dressed the way she dressed or said the things she said.

Well, she said, "Cigarette me, Big Boy." When Augie gave her one she said, "Thanks for nothing."

Then she sang "Redwing."

> For afar 'neath a star her brave lies sleeping
> While Redwing's weeping. . . .

But those were not the words she sang. The words she sang Doll had never heard said aloud, even in anger. Her skin grew hot and she was miserably afraid her embarrassment would be seen. They would know she understood the words, which is what embarrassed her. What's more, Duke laughed.

Before, he had been just as polite. True, while they drove up and down Higgins he had rested one hand behind her head so that unless she leaned way forward her hair brushed it. But what is wrong with that? And he had talked soberly of serious things. Whether Bozeman had a chance next fall against the School of Mines, and of his future: the minute he got out he was going to shake the dust from his heels. That didn't sound much like a small apartment, but young men change their minds. Once, in passing, she had mentioned Hilary's name and he had said, "Who?" That should not have been comforting, but it was. Sure she had let him kiss her. Before he drove off he had laughed, but in a nice way.

Tonight she did not think his laugh so nice.

Because Duke was taller and better looking, wouldn't you think that if anyone copied anyone, it would be Augie who copied Duke? But tonight whenever Augie laughed, Duke sniggered. Not a pretty word, but that's what it was. Sniggering.

One does not ask the fellow who plans the evening what he's planned. But in the back seat Augie and Marge slopped about in a way that was certainly up to them, but that made Doll hope whatever was planned did not entail riding under the streetlights much longer. Well, it didn't.

Before they got back to the Van Buren Bridge, Duke turned on Front Street. Left, not right. To the right on Front Street was where the whores hung out. Not that the girls were sure which ones were whores, but they had heard tell and could guess. It was said that the rooms over the butcher shop and the taxi stand and the shoe repair were all rented by whores, but the signs only said *Rooms* and if you see a person on the street it's hard to tell. She may be just a person with bad taste.

You know, Amelia had once told the kids that when she was very little her father had taken her up to one of those places and had introduced her to a woman whom he said was going to be her new mother just as soon as he and Anne were divorced; Amelia had had the funniest look as if she had just remembered that and wished she hadn't. Hilary said that children made up all sorts of stories, but that if she were Amelia she wouldn't tell that story anymore. And anyway, the Laceys had never been divorced.

On Front Street they passed the Bijou, which was the first theatre in town to have a talkie show. Everyone went, but there was not all that much talking in it, though Al Jolson did sing "Sonny Boy," so some felt cheated. Some did not.

They also passed the only grade school in town equipped to teach Domestic Science. Eighth grade you had to go way over there and learn to make white sauce. You had to eat it, too.

Doll thought it was a waste of time because way before eighth grade she was cooking all the meals and neither Aaron nor her father would eat plain white sauce on toast, which is the way you ate it in Domestic Science.

If you went on that way you reached the Van Buren Street Bridge and had to turn toward the University or leave town. Duke stopped before they got that far and said, "Everybody out."

There weren't so many streetlights in that part of town, and the place they stopped in front of was more like a shack. A pipe came out of it instead of a proper chimney and part of it was covered with tar paper.

Duke said, "We got a friend lives here."

Marge said, "Some friend."

It happened that the friend was just going out.

Doll had hoped that inside, it might turn out to be sort of cute, the kind of dollhouse that friends have when they marry too early and have to put up. But inside it was a dump. The friend was a wizened little man—if he had married too early it had been a long, long time ago. She had hoped for the bravery of matched cheap china, but nothing here matched and nothing had been washed. There was grease in the sink.

The friend winked. He said, "I prolly won't be back until way late. There's beer in the box."

Augie said, "There'd better be."

There was broken linoleum in the kitchen, a broken couch in the front room, and a broken lamp of twisted iron. There was a door to the one bedroom and another door to what should have been the bathroom but, as it turned out, wasn't. There was a radio. Duke brought the beer in big brown bottles.

Marge said, "Anyone got to have a glass?"

Any answer Doll made was not going to be the right answer

because Marge didn't like Doll and Doll knew it. If she asked for a glass, she was la-di-dah. Doll sort of liked home-brew, but she was not going to use any glass that had been near that sink and she was not going to tipple out of the bottle, either.

She said, "I guess I don't want any."

Duke said, "Maybe there's a Coke."

In Salt Lake City, it was the Bible Hour. A whole bunch of sugary young voices sang.

> I come to the garden alone
> When the dew is still on the roses. . . .

Marge said, "For God's sake, try Butte."

"Leave it on," Augie said. "It's a howl."

Doll was uncomfortable as she could be. Last year one day when Hilary had the car and there was nothing else to do, they had gone to look at the Holy Rollers. They wanted to see if they rolled. They didn't roll. They met in a small bare building with folding chairs.

Hilary said, "Nobody is to laugh."

Nobody laughed.

The girls had interrupted and when they went in, there was silence until they sat down. The people there were just quiet shabby folk. The minister, or whoever the head roller was, was a tired little man who looked a lot like Mr. Barry. He said, "Will you sing with us?"

> I come to the garden alone,
> When the dew is still on the roses. . . .

Hilary made them sit through the whole thing. She said, "I don't think it's funny."

Well, none of them thought that it was funny.

Now Marge snapped her blunt fingers. "Cigarette me," she said.

At some time, something had been spilled on the sofa cushions. Before she would rest Hilary's blouse against that sofa back, Doll put a cautious finger out. Whatever it was had dried. She sat down gingerly.

Then Augie said, "Come on, we're wasting time," and Marge giggled and Augie took her by her fat hand and they went through the door to the bedroom. First it was very silent in there, and then it wasn't. If they were petting in there, it was heavy petting.

It's hard to be told all your life not to be rude. You get into these situations and you'd like to get out of them, but how do you do it without being rude? If their idea was that they would all four hang around and pet, that was not Doll's idea. She didn't know Duke well enough to pet with him, and she was sore anyway because of what looked—for him—like a cheap evening. He hadn't even had to buy movie tickets, only to slip the friend something to clear out. It didn't say much for Doll if she was only worth a cheap evening.

He sat beside her and turned off the light without so much as a word. He smelled of a harsh after-shave. One thing she could say for her brother Aaron: he wouldn't be caught dead smelling like that.

Duke said, "Aah, baby."

She wasn't listening because she suddenly knew they were not petting in there. She didn't happen to give one toot what they did in there, but she didn't like it because they didn't care whether or not she gave a toot.

So Hilary was right and Duke was no damned good, because no fellow who is any good exposes you to that sort of thing unless you have invited it, and Doll could look Hilary straight in the face and swear that she had not invited it.

Or had she? She had let her hair brush his arm. Some would not take that for an invitation; apparently some do. Moreover, it might be an invitation in itself just to go out with anyone who was the best friend of Augie Spenelli.

Then Duke did two things that were so wrong that they made it all right for Doll to be rude.

He handed her a lighted cigarette and said, "I got to take a leak."

The lip of the cigarette was soaking wet and she did not want to touch his wetness. And while at home once in a while her own brother said that he was going to take a leak, that was entirely different. That was home and that was her own brother.

"Sure thing," Doll said brightly.

And then while Duke stumbled out the back door, she went out the front.

Before she got back to Higgins Avenue where it is safe, her pumps hurt. They had those skinny little heels that you can't balance on. Your stocking feet are not much more comfortable; besides, you have to carry the shoes. Between that awful shack and Higgins there were only three street lights with June-bugs bumping and shadows puddling around, but Doll was not afraid because a girl does not have to be afraid if she knows how far she is prepared to go and hasn't been prepared to go that far.

But she was glad to see Jon Powers' car idling along because little as she liked Jon she'd known him a long time and Hilary said he was all right.

"Boy," she said, "am I glad to see you."

"Mutual," he said. "Where's everyone?"

In the late light his face looked pinched. If he were in a gangster film, he wouldn't be the gangster. He would be the one who ratted. However, Hilary said he was all right. His mother played bridge with Janet's mother and his father had been a Sigma Chi, which meant that Jon was a legacy. They have to take you if you are a legacy, so being a legacy is both good and bad. You don't have to worry about being left out but you never know whether you would have been wanted anyway. In spite of Hilary, Doll had a feeling that Jon was lucky to be a legacy. If Jon had been well liked he wouldn't have been ditched tonight and he wouldn't have to ask, "Where's everyone?"

He said, "Want a ride?"

She said, "I sure do."

And Jon took her for a ride, all right. Way out of town and to the fairgrounds, where he stopped his car behind a billboard and attacked her.

But not very efficiently.

So neither one of them was any goddamned good. Doll wasn't one bit bruised or hurt but she was mad as hell and for a moment before she got hold of the high-heeled pump, she had been scared.

"What 'ja want to do that for?" he whimpered, groping for his broken glasses.

Doll said, "You figure it out."

Let him explain those glasses to his father.

But even as she hung up Hilary's ripped blouse, Doll cried because Hilary was right. It does matter, the way things look. There was no harm done, not yet, but she was never going to let it look again as if she had round heels.

Nobody heard her come in and nobody heard her slip into bed, and no one heard her cry. Anyway, she didn't cry all that long because that was not her way, and tomorrow was another day.

"Dumb bunny," Doll told Doll.

Live and learn.

18

In the morning, they were all cross as two sticks. Thanks to Hilary, they were out of harm's way; their names would not be bandied about. She did not expect them to be grateful, but she did expect them to show more pep. All they did was complain.

They hadn't known the nights were going to be so cold. They hadn't thought of breakfast—first, you must have your fire. It was nice of whoever had stacked the firewood, but there was no kindling. Not one of them was going to split kindling. Suppose the ax should slip? Did Hilary know how to apply a tourniquet? Well, then.

And Janet, who knew these things because her father was the doctor, said if you did it wrong you would bleed to death and if you did it right, gangrene would follow. No, they were not going to split kindling.

Kathy had brought raisin bread but no one had remembered to bring butter. And what good is toast without a toaster? A mosquito had bitten Kathy on the eyelid. The eye was swollen shut and looked a fright. What difference did it make what Kathy looked like, Hilary wanted to know? There wasn't a male in miles.

Amelia moved about nervously.

Hilary bit the ball of her thumb. She was puzzled. It seemed to her that Amelia was acting oddly. She might, of course, be worried about her mother; Hilary thought her concern for Anne excessive, but conceded that concern is a price one pays. Well, a good organizer organizes. The morning buzzed with insects, the surface of the lake was scattered with gold coins, and the last one in was a rotten egg.

Kathy said, "Does my eye look better?"

"No," Hilary told her.

When you get right down to it there is not much to do out of doors, once you have had your swim. You can bake in the sun until you get as brown as an Indian, but nobody in Montana wants to be brown as an Indian. In California they bake in the sun. Hilary had seen pictures of starlets who, before they baked, had taped to their backs the silhouette of the Blue Eagle. It was an interesting idea. But in Montana girls stayed covered up.

What do you suppose the starlets do about their evening gowns? So far, the girls had not required evening gowns. Once a year Edna Macpherson gave a private dance to which they were not invited, but they understood that the girls went bare-backed and the boys rented monkey suits. For the occasion, the Macphersons rented the tearoom called the Blue Parrot. Hilary had long wanted to be a hostess at the Blue Parrot, but had the wit not to suggest it. The rent for the one night was fifty dollars.

But next spring they would all need evening gowns, and much as Hilary respected Mr. Barry—and she did, she did!—she was not going to go to the Kappa House with the Blue Eagle on her back.

All things considered, it seemed good to row across the lake. They could get butter. They could also take a look at the wrong sort of people over there. Failing that, they could stay here in the shade of the tamaracks and discuss crime.

Morbidity is normal. Consider the little pigs, otherwise law-abiding, who boiled the wolf. How the little ones clap! And the old witch who is pushed into the oven. And for that matter, the parents who left the children in the woods where the old witch could get them. Later on, there are kidnappers; the very least they do is cut you up in little pieces. It must be true, because your parents stop the newspapers. If it's not true, why do they stop the papers?

Still later you see that in your own town, bad things happen. All around you, people destroy themselves in ingenious ways; sometimes you are familiar with the street they lived on. Presumably, this marks the heyday of your interest, though it is understood that some people never outgrow that interest, painters and writers and such-like. There you are. Hired men run amok, estranged husbands and wives shoot it out, perfectly respectable men are found hanging in the barn. The dentist's wife takes drugs.

And just this spring that rabbity pair of kids at Missoula County High had something frightful happen. They looked much alike, as kids who start going steady early often do; they were both blond and had pale eyes and pink noses. Well, they were driving home late one night and there was an old bum in the road and they hit him and he died. They had to go to court. There was a certain amount of talk because the neighbors said her father didn't like the boy and maybe the boy thought it was the father in the road. But the judge said it was an accident.

Janet said, "It's my father's opinion that neither one of them are all there."

"Oh, for cat's sake."

Even Janet ought to remember that Amelia's own little sister was not all there.

Amelia got up and left them.

"Somebody's got to get kindling," she said.

"Did I say something wrong?" Janet asked.

Then they heard the dull crashing of the ax.

Hilary drew a stalk of timothy across her lips. It tickled. She was worried about Amelia, who, if she went overboard, might turn against her friends or even go back East to school. Why did Amelia's eyes slide so uneasily and why did her white fingers comb her black hair? It seemed to Hilary that she was unnaturally immune to disasters. She did not want to talk about the dentist's wife. She did not want to hear of Mr. Barry. She had once left the room when Kathy spoke of Oscar Wilde.

"So," Hilary said, "suppose we row across the lake?"

Janet said it was a long way over there; she herself had never been much of a rower and they might get blisters.

Kathy preferred that nobody see her eye.

Amelia said that she was not going to row over there today or any other day and that it was quite possible that she would never cross the lake again. Hilary told Amelia to get hold of herself and Amelia burst into tears and then Janet pulled up the leg of her pants and screamed.

She had a tick.

It was embedded in the fat of her thigh, its hard little head was way out of sight and its legs wiggled. Not one of them knew what to do. Not one!

Amelia said angrily, "We don't have ticks up here." And then because they looked at her, she said, "Not the bad ones."

Who is to know the bad one?

Janet was whimpering, as anyone would do with an insect in her. She said, "I want my father."

That was reasonable, since Janet's father was also her medical man. Hilary sighed with relief. She said, "So of course you've had the shots."

"No," Janet said, "I haven't. My father's been too busy."

Well, then! Her father was lax and her friends faithless.

"Anyway," Hilary said, and she hoped it helped, "if there's any damage, the damage has been done."

It did not seem to comfort. Janet still preferred not to have an insect buried in her own self. One thing they all did know was what you were not to do. You were not to pull because only the body came, not the head, which had already entered. All little girls despise anything that enters.

Amelia said, "I have heard kerosene?"

They had all heard kerosene. What had skipped their attention was what you were supposed to do with the kerosene. Perhaps when drenched, the tick would back out? Because setting ticks afire did not sound practical. Janet wanted to go home. But, Hilary pointed out, it took days for Spotted Fever to incubate, and in the meantime . . . ? Janet still wanted to go home. Little as her father cared for her, if she was incubating, she would rather incubate near her father.

All right. But since Janet had no fever yet, Amelia wanted to close up her mother's place and properly. How long was that going to take? Long enough so that they would have to drive in the dark . . . suppose they ran out of gas?

Amelia said they were not going to run out of gas.

What if they got a flat?

Well, what if? But Amelia said that whatever they decided was all right with her as long as it was understood that she would not abandon her mother's property without properly closing up. However long that took would depend on how useful they all made themselves.

Janet cried quietly now, but persistently. She said she certainly couldn't help. She said she had not expected to come all the way up to Little Bear Lake to learn to hate her dearest friends. She said she felt sort of pale. They looked closely. She did look sort of pale.

Nobody wanted to inspect the tick.

"I understand they drop off," Hilary said. "Eventually."

Nobody wished to consider why it was that they fell off. Eventually.

Amelia said, "Why don't you pull your pants leg down?"

That hurt Janet's feelings.

So Hilary said it was time to get the whiskey out. And then in case Amelia thought she was getting away with anything, she added sternly, "What there is left of it."

So ended the first lesson.

19

When Hank Hunter first began to wonder if it was time he started to worry about Hilary, he decided to let Myra do it. Mothers are more efficient worriers. Although he surely did not know in this world why they should worry about either of the kids. They were both able-bodied.

But Myra brought up things that hadn't occurred to Hank. She said that she herself was married when she was not all that much older than Hilary was right now. She said the little Barry boy looked peaked. She also wanted to take the Barrys out for a drive. What good was that going to do? And then she said that Hilary was still just a little girl and although she, as her mother, firmly believed that someday Hilary would be sensible, she was not sensible right now.

Then having put the worry back on Hank, Myra perked right up.

So when Hilary came home before they expected her and what's more, too late at night, naturally he got sore.

But Hilary was also sore, which was great, because though he could see something had gone wrong, he could also see she wouldn't be sore if it were anything a father had to think about. In the pink light of the front hall, her hair looked very red.

He said, "I suppose it never occurred to you that your mother might have gone to bed?"

She glared right back. She said, "Why do you think it's time I had a key?"

What next?

He knew damn well what next. The blood rose to his temples, which was not comfortable and, as Myra said, not even safe.

But to see the kid both safe and fresh was too much. His hands clenched his hips.

And then, above, his wife was there in one of those long shapeless things that were so warm and felt so good.

"Now see what you've done," Hank said to Hilary. "We woke your mother."

He never used to be hotheaded until he went Over There. When Hank had first gone over there he had never been afraid of anything in his whole life: or so he said. Many things people say are not true. As a boy he had been afraid of grizzly bears, but that is sensible. Then when he had the measles a nice neighbor told him that he would probably go blind.

And then, there was that Indian.

But on the whole he had been a spunky kid and an even-tempered young man who, once he had seen Myra and had felt the soft cushions of her wrists, spoke right up.

"Be nice to her," her father said.

"Sure thing," Hank told him. "Bet your boots."

He had, too.

Back then being from the West was still different from being from the East, or from anyplace else where they just happened to talk United States. Everyone knew there was a war in Europe, but that was the other side of the world and had nothing to do with Montana. You wouldn't even have known how Europe was supposed to sound if Miss Haggerty hadn't said, because it sure doesn't look the way it is supposed to sound. And then all those foreigners dressed up and shooting one another. In this day and age.

Meanwhile Myra, with her pretty hair wrapped in a cloth, dusted everything.

Then it all happened overnight.

One day we were minding our own business and the next, we were spoiling for a fight. They never learn that, over there. The good old U.S.A. drew a circle with its toe and said you dassn't, and by God, the Kaiser dass't. He sank the *Reuben James* and then he sank the *Lusitania*, and the fat was in the fire. Congress got sore as hell because the folks at home were sore. The ladies started rolling bandages and selling bonds and handing out white feathers.

🎖 UNCLE SAM WANTS YOU, and everywhere you went, Uncle Sam pointed at you; he meant Hank.

Naturally he hated to leave Myra, who was pregnant and cried a lot until he explained that it was not going to be dangerous, not in the cavalry. Then she cheered up and he got the feeling that she would rather be with her mother anyway, as long as it was not dangerous in the cavalry. She didn't even seem to mind as much as he did the closing up of that small house and the removal of their few sundries.

Her father shook him heavily by the hand and looked straight in his eyes. The women were in the kitchen at the time.

And then there were the songs. "The Yanks Are Coming"; here he came. There was another one that he didn't like very much.

> Keep your head down, Fritzi Boy—
> You were seen last night in the pale moonlight
> I saw you—I *saw you*. . . .

That one made him uncomfortable.

> You were mending the broken wire
> When we opened rapid fire. . . .

You see, it reminded him that those fellows were fellows, too.

However, he did like the puttees and the overseas cap—he was very partial to the cap—and he liked the pictures in the newspapers of fellows grinning in those caps; they also waved. By the time he possessed a cap like that he would be far from home and would have to grin at strangers who, if they saved the newspaper at all would save it only because there they were themselves on the corner of the platform. Still, a young man who has never been out of state does like to get out of state. And while he was not himself personally interested in any of them, he did want to see the mademoiselles and taste the wines and see if it was true that the wine came in leather bags the way—right in Idaho—the Basques carry wine. Besides, there wasn't an able-bodied American man who didn't want to tell the Kaiser what he could do.

As it turned out, the war was not what it was cracked up to be. The mademoiselles were hairy, the army food was bad and the French food—well, if they were doing it for Hank they could stop anytime. The cavalry was safe enough, God knows, because there wasn't any cavalry. The cavalry cleaned up after the mules and when the mules were dragging the big guns out of the mud, the cavalry cleaned spark plugs. None of it was what Hank had expected, not at all.

Moreover, like any westerner, he didn't like to be told what to do. He could take a suggestion well as the next—but an order! And from any shavetail, too. But that was how you had to do it.

For some time he was stationed in a small town where several Americans were quartered in the home of a whiskery woman who, of the goodness of her heart, watched out for their linens and their morals. When from sheer boredom any of them wandered away and came back reeking, she turned the pictures of their wives and sweethearts to the wall. Myra never was turned to the wall; when Hank was bored he walked a lot and read her letters.

The mail was slow. When it did come, it came in bunches. No matter how you love someone, if that someone is a quiet living person there is a certain similarity in her accounts of that quiet life. If it comes in bunches. One thing he liked about his wife was that she permitted him to direct her, but when he had directed her not to worry about him, he had not meant it as literally as she took it. While he was still in the states, her letters were almost too cheerful.

So much so that the night before he left Fort Dix he wrote to her, "Off to the Front!"

She bore it very well.

The only thing about which he had not been able to alleviate her anxiety was the cold—she was persuaded that he spent his days in trenches and in puddles, and his nights in drafty dugouts. So she knitted for him socks, mittens, underwear (not very comfortable), and helmets. Many women knitted helmets for their men and some men wore them, out of loyalty. They looked like those chain metal ones Crusaders wore, although for the most part the women made them of brown wool. Hank could not wear Myra's helmets even for loyalty because, having all that yarn left over from the baby, they were pink.

But up until this time he had not been afraid.

Then came a night when he waited, not at the front, but closer to the front than he cared to be, and not in a trench but in a small railroad station that should have been abandoned but was not. There was much confusion. The place the Allies were supposed to hold was held by the enemy; a few miles ahead they were all shooting it out. Hank heard the grumble of the guns and saw the green pulsing of the Very flares, like northern lights at home.

Enemy. The word made him ill at ease, as if he was in the presence of something excessive. Naturally Hank had run into those who didn't like him and had not liked them back. But it would never have occurred to him to hurt them—to question their worth or let the air out of their tires. Let alone blow them up. It was unlikely that he himself would be blown up tonight—that would take a stray shell and a direct hit. Chances were against.

But he was scared, a feeling that was new to him, and unpleasant. By God, he *did* have enemies, thousands of enemies, any one of whom would kill him if they could. Why, they would smash him to a pulp, and if they did, who was going to look after his wife? Because Myra was the best woman in the world, but without sense enough to pound sand into a rat hole. And who would care for the child she was going to bear him?

Oh, don't give him that. Her folks were old, the government didn't give a damn, and the help of strangers is cold comfort. The herd does not protect the orphan. He had seen what happens to the eweless lamb—the coyote gets it. And he had seen bum calves with their eyes picked out: you hoped they'd died before the magpies came.

Somebody's lucky shot took down a pole or a transformer and the bad lights went out. In the hissing light of the Coleman lantern Hank saw that he was not the only one who was scared. A couple of the guys started clowning around; a certain kind of fellow feels better if he's clowning around. It never was Hank's way. He lit a Gauloise that about took out his throat, and threw it down and stepped on it.

No—Hank was probably all right this time, this night. But up there they were getting theirs: winners and losers both, smashed, blinded, dead. It was a world where that could happen. Behind him, a big Bohunk from the mines started to sing dirty.

"Knock it off," Hank suggested.

He didn't, personally, care one way or the other, though he had never got in the habit of dirty talk, himself. But there was an Irish kid who went to Carroll College over by Helena and hoped to go to seminary, and that kid was uncomfortable.

You hear a lot of dirty talk in bunkhouses, and bunkhouses made him think of his Dad, and his Dad made him think of the Indian.

Hank's father was a patient man and people trusted him. The year that Hank was eight his father was working for this fellow had a little spread out of Rosebud. One time the fellow had to be away and asked Hank's father would he move into the house to look after. That was a good time. After the supper dishes they would sit by the stove.

"We got it pretty good," his father said.

One gray November morning there was a knock at the front door.

People on ranches don't like knocks on the front door because anyone who belongs comes in the back. And because Hank knew about ambushes and scalpings and slivers under your fingernails, of course he was scared of Indians. But he was surprised that his father was scared, too.

How could a grown man be afraid of such an old Indian? But he could smell his father's fear. The Indian was so old that his eyes dropped into their sockets. He looked sick. His shoes were busted up and his braids were thin. He said he hadn't eaten and he asked for food.

Hank's Dad said no.

The old Indian whined and persisted and Hank's father, who never was mad, got mad and lifted his voice. The Indian turned and stumbled from the porch. They watched him wander up the road, the thin braids moving in the wind.

And then Hank's father turned on Hank. He said, "Got nothing better to do than stand and gawk?" And he caught him hard against the backside.

Later he said, "If it had been my own place. See?"

Later, Hank knew his father was not afraid of the Indian. His father was afraid of poverty and age and not being able to help those who are in need.

Then the big Bohunk started up again.

> Mademoiselle from Armentières
> Hasn't been. . . .

and Hank saw red. Rage, like the hot bite of good liquor. "Shut your goddamned dirty mouth!"

The Bohunk did shut his dirty mouth. But that was not what counted. What counted was the way he knew suddenly that any

Kraut who came after Hank Hunter was going to be one sorry Kraut. So after that when Hank got frightened he got mad, because that is safer. Except for once.

That was when he first met the stern, redheaded little girl who didn't even know him.

20

THE BLACK-HAIRED BOY was the funniest fellow. Practically the first thing he said to Doll was, "I can't take you out anytime except on Sundays."

Who said he was going to take her out at all? He did.

She was hurrying across the bridge on a day that wasn't meant to be hurried in; the sun hung like a hot penny. Later, it would thunder. She was late. Her father had thought it just the day for a pork roast, and pork takes time. The pickup ambled by, and sure enough, on the other side of the bridge the boy was waiting.

Hilary had always, always said never take a ride unless you truly know the fellow. And she had explained that it was not so much that it was dangerous (although it was dangerous) but that it was not ladylike.

Hilary said, "Do you think my mother would let a fellow pick her up?"

Well, no.

But you can't call someone a stranger when you have been aware of him all year long in study hall. And once you have considered his ill-chosen shoes, you are acquainted. She clambered to the cab.

"Whew," she said. "Thanks."

"Sure thing," he said.

His eyes stayed straight ahead. His hand moved on the gear. His hand was huge, the fingers long, the nails immaculate, which told you quite a lot. The sweat that beaded his forehead smelled sweet.

Doll said, "I'll tell you where to turn."

He said, "I know where to turn."

What do you know!

Doll never was surprised when the fellows liked her, because she liked the fellows. If you like people they usually like you back. That didn't mean she meant to go out with him. However, when he pulled up in front of the little house on Hilda Avenue she said, "All right." And then she said, "How come?"

Oh, hot.

Over Mount Jumbo bruised and swollen clouds bumped together. On her father's lawn there was a little poplar tree: all its coin-shaped leaves rattled. Doll put her hands under her soft dark hair and lifted it so that the damp wind stroked her nape. "I mean," she said, "most everyone gets off Saturday night."

"Saturday night my Dad comes to town. Somebody's got to stay on the place."

That didn't tell her whether the place was a farm or ranch, but it did tell her that the place was small. That meant this boy wasn't suitable. Not for a girl who was looking to the future.

Doll did not intend to be one of those country wives who come to town with their worn heels and shapeless dresses to wander wistfully the aisles of J.C. Penney's admiring the cardboard purses and the papery hats. And she had cooked about as much as she cared to cook. To wrestle with a wood range, take slops to the pig, and shovel food to extra hands at harvest or at haying? Scour the roasting pans, the separator, the worn kettles with thin bottoms in which turnips boiled?

Not Doll.

"By the way," she said to the black-haired boy, "I don't know your name."

"It's Con. Short for Cornelius."

He scowled as if he thought that she might smile, but Doll saw nothing funny about Cornelius. Her mother had said that Irishmen make good husbands if you can catch them. They are not partial to the notion but, once caught, they are true and faithful. Some of them make very little money and some make a lot, but almost none of them ever light out.

"And so," he said, "I will pick you up at about two o'clock. That ought to give you time to do the dishes."

Sometime when she knew him better Doll was going to explain that on the whole, women would rather be asked than told. At the moment, for some reason, it did not annoy her. The cab of the pickup smelled sort of like oilcloth. She did wonder how he planned to entertain her, and couldn't for the life of her see why she shouldn't ask; it makes a great deal of difference in the way you dress. If what he had in mind was the movies, she could wear her heels.

One reason you don't ask is that the boy may not yet know. A lot depends upon how much he can scrape up. But Doll hoped it wouldn't be the movies. You sit there and he sits there and afterward, even if you held hands, you don't know him any better than you did before. In the shank of the afternoon the light is drab, you ache from sitting still, and if either of you is going to snap, that's when you do it.

As she watched the old truck rattle off, it occurred to Doll that she didn't give a fig whether Hilary was watching or not. She would love Hilary always and Hilary would always love her. The friendship was over.

Someone was watching from across the street, but it was Myra. She rather liked what she saw. The desperate old truck looked honest. The tires were worn, but no collision had insulted those good fenders. It was an honest working vehicle and not for joyrides. She couldn't see the boy very clearly except to see that he was dark and tall, but before Doll climbed down from the cab this boy got out, walked around and opened the door for her. Why, Myra hadn't seen anyone do that for years!

It made her feel good.

Lately there had not been much to feel good about. When she stopped to think about it, she remembered that for some time now Hank had teased her about stumbling; her ankles turned easily. "Graceful as a cow," he said, and always added, "but prettier."

Lately she lost her balance even if there was nothing there to stumble over. Then the eggs began to drop, and then more precious things.

"Butterfingers!" she would say gaily.

But when she was alone she mourned the Sèvres cup, the Wedgwood saucer, the recalcitrant hands that would not do her bidding.

Yesterday she had taken the first fall.

She had gone down cellar, her arms laden with jars of wild gooseberry jam. Coming back, on the first step she fell. A person of her size falls hard. She did believe for a moment she was quite knocked out. When she came to she was frightened. Anyone would be. Then she lay thinking of all she had to be thankful for. In the first place no one was at home, so there was no one to be scared or startled. Then too, if she had fallen going down, she would have lost all the gooseberry jam.

After a few moments more she tried, gingerly. Nothing was broken.

Today the big lump on her head hurt very much when she touched it, but it didn't show. However, hot as the day was she had to wear long sleeves, because if any of them saw her bruised and battered arm, there'd be no end to it.

So in all fairness, something had to be done.

21

From time to time, Myra came out with the darndest things. The others were used to her innocencies. "Gee whillikers," she said. Or someone was hornswoggled. These did not offend. But sometimes she swung easily into a later speech and referred to something as the "bees' knees" or the "cat's meow." Or if someone courteously questioned the state of her being, she would say, "Dunt esk."

At such times Hilary and her father would not look at one another, and her son left the room and went upstairs.

When the doctor made what seemed to him a reasonable, indeed an imperative, suggestion, this plump surprising woman with her sensible shoes and great pretty eyes said, "Not on your tintype."

He was accustomed to women and to their several reactions to this particular suggestion, was often met with tears or hysteria or even anger, however misplaced, but he was not accustomed to what amounted to simple civil disobedience.

He looked at her in disbelief.

She looked right back.

"Besides," she said, "professional men should not jump to conclusions."

The lack of logic! It was precisely why he wanted tests—because he was not jumping to conclusions. Precisely why!

"Madam," he said, "You came to consult me. Not I you."

Myra, who tried to be fair-minded, sighed. He was right. But she was not used to consulting any doctor. When Dan was born and when he broke his leg, they had had dear old Dr. Temple in. He brought the baby and he set the leg, but he did not consult with them or they with him. Since Dr. Temple died the Hunters had not happened to need any doctor, so when Myra had decided she must see someone, she really and truly did not know where to turn. But this man's little girl was a friend of her own little girl and a nice child too, so presumably her father would be friendly and would tell Myra something, well—friendly.

Since it had not turned out that way, she did not want him to feel bad about it. Still, what he suggested was impossible. The *hospital*? Hank was quite worried enough, what with his present business and all his future plans about which she was not supposed to know. She wasn't that ill and didn't intend to be.

So she said, wanting the doctor to feel better, "I'll tell you what." She had always found that a useful phrase. "I'll think it over and you think it over and then I'll come back and we'll see what we think."

At that, he had the last word. "Don't be too long about it," the doctor said.

After she left he tapped his teeth with his pencil. How could he be sure? But he thought it was one of the scleroses. If it was, there was nothing at all that he could do. When the nerve ends degenerate, they degenerate. This posed a pretty problem. No, there wasn't anything he could do for Mrs. Hunter. He could do nothing for any child with poliomyelitis. No one could do anything about cancer.

Some day they would be able. It wasn't long ago when no one could do anything for Spotted Fever.

But you have to have tests, you have to have observation, you have to have controlled data. This Mrs. Hunter seemed a nice woman, though mad. Perhaps if he came right out?

No.

Some say you should tell the patient and some say you shouldn't. As far as Janet's father was concerned, he couldn't.

You could not get a cab in Missoula, not without stealth and foresight. Anyone who did not wish to use the perfectly adequate bus must walk. If for some reason you insisted, you were to telephone the office, a narrow storefront next to the shoe repair, and one of the young men who sporadically worked there would probably take you where you wanted to go.

Myra, with the permission of the nurse, made such a call. And then downstairs she waited in the damp vestibule and peered anxiously into the street, not because it was raining (although it was raining) but because in a town no bigger than Missoula, who knows what friends or relatives may pass by.

It made her mad as hops that she was not allowed to drive. Everyone else had learned—why not Myra? Why, even Dan could drive, though only when Hank had the time to take him to the fairgrounds, where they went solemnly around the racecourse. But when she suggested that she, too, would like to drive, the three of them just looked at her.

Therefore she waited, damp and defensive. And why defensive, she would like to know? Because the guilty flee where no man pursues. That she, of all people, should bring grief to her loved ones?

Creatures are sad and vulnerable in the rain. All over Montana, that bad day, it rained. The rain washed the blood from the slaughter pens and clawed the dirt roads. In sodden pastures the horses turned disconsolate backs. Chickens drooped. Cows mourned. The foothills, like widows, were swathed in black shawls.

And here on Silver Street great drops plopped on the gritty sidewalk. Pretty soon the gutters would run with soiled water, carrying gum wrappers like small gay boats. Then the water would rush beneath the bridge, hurling debris against that small sandy island; from the upper floors of the Wilma Building a few miscreants would hurl some debris of their own. Among the bottles, rotted paper crates, smashed branches, who could identify what the hurler hurled?

The stench from the sugar beet factory hung low. Across the street two Indians huddled under a dripping awning, their blankets swaddled close.

But dry in her own house again, Myra felt better. Why, looky here. She was a strong woman who had twice given birth without turning a hair. That is what Dr. Temple said to Hank—she heard him. He said, "She didn't turn a hair."

Hank had said, "Oh, thank God."

Then he had looked at Dan.

He said, "That's some boy. Isn't that some boy?"

Dr. Temple said that was certainly some boy.

What's more, she was a strong young woman. Forty is young.

She put her hat (the unimportant one) in the hall closet and hung her raincoat in the back entry—if anyone asked why it was damp, she was going to say Hilary must have worn it. The fact was that she didn't get out enough and from now on might very well go out more often.

The rain which had buffeted and brawled now slid gently down the window panes and the lamp dropped a warm yellow pool upon the table. A lemon pie cooled on its rack and the meringue stood high and fluffy and beaded with amber sugar. The kettle purred, and Myra thought about the letter.

Like many happy women who are not yet in any danger, Myra had given a good deal of thought to what her children would think of her when she was gone. To make sure what they thought, she had spent many pleasant hours in writing them a long loving letter filled with wise advice. Upon the envelope she had written "To be opened when I am gone." But she had never sealed the envelope since she often wished, and needed, to add to it and to revise. She hid the letter because if it were found too soon, the good would be gone. And also, Hank would laugh.

Myra liked to hide things and felt that she was a good hider. Take Easter eggs; the balance is delicate. If they are found too easily there is no fun in it. Still, one does wish them found. An Easter egg is not attractive if it does not show up till Christmas— that other hiding time. Myra felt she had solved the problem of the letter well.

There was in the upstairs hall a special closet which was, for the most part, dedicated to her husband. There he kept his things for hunting and fishing and his gum-boots and such. Up on the shelf Myra kept a large hatbox that was plainly labeled HAT. Inside there really was a hat, one so beribboned and beveled and becoming that all understood why she did not want to part with it, and since no one else in the house required such a hat, Myra kept her letter there.

In all these years, she had only had one fright. That was when Hilary volunteered the hat to the Thespians, who were performing something that could use a hat. Myra had caught Hilary tiptoe and red-handed, although of course the child had no idea that she would mind. And of course if it had only been the hat, she wouldn't have minded. She had to pretend an unaccustomed pique.

"No, no!" she cried. "They may not have my hat!" She even stamped a little.

"All right," her daughter said.

"They would get greasepaint on it," Myra told her. "I wouldn't take your hat, without I asked."

Sometimes when she did not feel the call to write, Myra fell back on the words of other people. Authors do have that knack. Well, look:

Trust thyself. Every heart vibrates to that iron string.

That was well put!

And once in a while she wrote things down just because they tickled her.

In the spring time, the spring time,
The only pretty ring time,
When lovers sing hey-ding a ding ding!
Sweet lovers love the spring.

Though honest and truly, she did not see how that was going to help the children. There was another verse she had never written down, so she would never have to strike it out.

> Western wind, when will thou blow
> That the small rain down can rain?
> Christ that my love were in my arms
> And I in my bed again.

But you can't tell your children that kind of thing; you can only pray that one day they will feel that way. When the time comes.

And there were certain helpful hymns she wished them to remember.

> Someone far from harbor you may guide across the bar;
> Brighten the corner where you are!

The little girls were always after her to sing that one, and then they would double up. But someday they would see how true it is and what sage counsel, since those who brighten corners are well liked.

She had never run across any author great enough to tell you how to die.

But Myra did not intend to die; she just wished she had used a lick of sense and found a better doctor. Mrs. Barry had been wild about the one who took out her gallbladder. She had no words good enough. If Myra did go to another doctor, though probably she would not, she would shop around and find one who made you feel better. Isn't that what you pay for? Meantime, she would have to get the letter out again, because there were a lot of important things she hadn't told them yet.

No, she would not be sick. It wasn't fair to Hank. And having settled that, she began to think of dinner. She just happened to have a goose. She had bought it for Sunday, but Sunday might be quite a different sort of day: goose goes well with rain and applesauce. She happened also to have apples.

Maybe Doll would like to join them.

And while she had the letter out, it did seem to her that Hilary would like to have her recipe for the goose stuffing.

Anybody would.

22

ANNE LACEY WOULDN'T HAVE been seen dead downtown with that fellow and that being so, she shouldn't have let him come around at all. But he amused her. It had been a long time since she had been amused.

The first time he showed up, Anne was in a rotten mood. If she had any virtue of which she was proud (some people didn't seem to think that she had any virtues) it was that when she was in a rotten mood, she admitted. Mrs. Phelps said Anne had to mind the child herself. Amelia was away and Spud off doing something somewhere he could just as well have put off.

Anne didn't like to mind the child and never had. They all knew it. Apparently what she liked or didn't like was, to them, a matter of indifference.

She sat by the swimming pool. The child was somewhere roundabout. Another year she might not have the pool filled at all, and then the child could run around without all this watching, no matter what the others said. But she herself liked to swim; it was a problem. She liked to swim and she liked to drive because both gave her a sense of power: *Here I come.* Amelia was always nagging about her mother's driving fast, but it was all right for Anne to drive fast because she didn't drink. If an antelope sprang into her road or a cow lumbered, she could stop on a dime. Apart from swimming and driving fast, she had damn little fun.

She glanced up and here this fellow was.

After a moment she said, "What do you want?"

He let her wait while his pale eyes caught her directly. Then he said, "Brought you something."

Of course she was startled, but any fear she felt was slight and pleasurable. He was male, he was young, but not too young, and he was different. He wore his hands buckled on his belt. Those pale eyes were far too shrewd for a crazy man. She crossed her narrow ankles. The wide legs of her linen lounging pajamas fell away gracefully.

She said, "If you'd had the courtesy to call, I might have let you in the usual way."

He grinned. He said, "Then again, you mightn't."

He wore jeans and boots and the obligatory hat, but she couldn't place him. His clothes were too cheap for a businessman playing cowboy, and too new for a real one.

"Look here," Anne said, "do you work for me?"

"No," he said. "Can I sit down?"

Why not? Nothing was going to happen to a rich woman within calling distance of her own housekeeper. "Because if you did," she said, "I don't have anything to do with all of that. Will you have a drink?"

"I don't drink much," he said.

She shrugged. That was up to him. She moved her head quickly so that the black bright hair fell across one eye. Then with a ringed hand (her rings were nice) she tossed it back.

"Well then," she said. "How did you get in?"

He said, "It wasn't hard."

Probably not. The gates were not intended to keep people out, but one small person in. Anyone could scale the fence, but most people do not care to be seen scaling. She had a feeling that this fellow didn't give a damn what anybody saw him do. She rather liked that.

Then he said, "They told me you were a good-looking woman."

There, he took the wrong tack. She was not flattered by the phrase because she was pretty sure she knew what he considered a good-looking woman. She did not fill the bill. Although it had been useful all her life to be thought naive, it also annoyed her. She lowered her lashes and, beneath them, assessed him coldly.

He was muscled and tall but something about him was not nice. His hands were bad: coarse, heavy knuckled, with short thick nails. Also, his hands were hairy. Anne never had liked hairy men.

He was low class.

And now he said, "You got a pretty kid there, too."

Anne Lacey's daughter should not even be noticed by one like this one.

She said coldly, "You've met my daughter?"

"Just the once. At the lake."

There was a brief thrashing in the bushes behind the pool and he whirled around. The child, like an animal, scuttered and crouched. She stared at them. Then she turned and ran on her stick-legs. At the next clump of bushes she stooped and vanished. The branches rattled and then quieted.

This man said, "Creepy."

Anne said, "She also is my daughter."

He said, "I heard say."

"Get out of here," she said.

"Oh sure, I'm going."

With the child gone, that raw insouciance returned. His smile was foxy, narrow and white.

"Whyn'ch you let me say first why I came?"

A thin cloud twitched the sun from her shoulders. From the fraternity house a block away she heard the young at play. Oh, God, she was bored. Pretty soon Mrs. Phelps would have to feed the child and then she could be put to bed.

Her gaze was challenging as his. "Why should I let you say anything?" she asked. "I don't know you from Adam."

"Ah," he said. "But you will."

That is how it began, if you can say that anything that amounted to so little began. What he wanted was bizarre, but not impossible. He liked her cabin. He was tired of bunking at Groveland and would rather cross the lake after hours so he could have some peace and quiet. In return, he would care for the cabin.

"Ask the kid if I didn't do it good," he said. "Opening up."

Her eyes flew wide. Nobody had asked him to open up. "And how did you know when?"

He shrugged. "I heard somebody say."

That was not true. No one had known the girls were coming. She should have been furious that anyone should use her property for his own purposes. She would, of course, put an end to that. But for the moment she found his audacity entertaining, if only because it would be rather fun to reduce that rampant confidence.

"Of course," he offered, "I'd move out any time you wanted."

Nice of him.

"Meantime," he said, "the place needs paint. Screens mended. Such. I think there's rot in the porch."

Anne had always known you could get away with a good deal if you had brass enough. His words were respectful, his eyes impertinent.

"You won't want to make up your mind right off the bat. But you could get in touch. Or . . ." Maybe he didn't dare. But he did dare. "You ever go to the Red Rooster?"

"No," she said.

For a moment his eyes were not nice. Then he said mildly, "Well, of course. A lady."

So that was settled there and then. She would not be seen with him. Anyplace. Ever.

He said, "But halfway up to Little Bear? There's a place nobody knows either."

Anne knew that place. A rattail bar sour with beer where a few local hands hung out. Terrible old trucks with thin tires stopped there and once in a while, somebody's cook.

"Joey's," he said. "Matter of fact, it would be easier for me."

To her surprise, she laughed. The sound rang strangely through the ragged garden. He looked about him critically. "You could use help here too," he said. "Getting too much for the old geezer?"

"Feel free to leave by the gate," she told him, "just like other people. The old geezer will let you out."

He grinned. "The question is," he said, "who's going to let me in."

When he had gone she sat listening to the silence. The water in the pool lay flat and stale. A small leaf, sered before its time, floated there uncircling and not a blade of disordered grass stirred. Beyond the black iron fence a horn honked, faintly. What was she to do to fill the rest of this blank day? Or the next, or the next, or the next?

She did meet him at Joey's, and more than once. Nobody at home knew where she went; she had always kept her own counsel, and Spud and Amelia were used to it. On her fast lonely drives she never had told them when to expect her back. If she began accounting for herself, there would be no end to it.

Joey himself was a cadaverous type who had apparently accepted his inability to think well of anyone. Anne was sure when he sized them up he had decided that one or both of them were married. Why, except for illicit purposes, would anyone meet at his bar? But believe me, Anne Lacey was doing nothing wrong. The game was innocent as a child's—thrust and parry. Spud would think it foolhardy because she didn't know anything about the man, but Spud was an old woman; always had been. And trying to find out about Earl was half the fun.

She suspected that he probably was married or had been, and had perhaps dissolved the tie by simply walking out. At a certain level many westerners marry casually and often; she knew he was a westerner because in the East people who are low class have quite a different speech. She could not make out in which western state he was wanted, but she was sure from his wariness and secrecy that he was wanted by some sheriff or creditor or, perhaps, by the abandoned wife. He wouldn't tell her anything: neither where he had come from nor where he was headed.

He never asked her anything about herself, but then he didn't have to. Everyone in the state knew all about the Laceys.

The bar was dark and damp; all day the tall trees shouldered it from the sun, and the tall-backed booth where they sat was private as a cave. Anne supposed there was an outside chance that someone driving to Little Bear might drop in, but not for a drink— nobody needs a drink that bad. It would be an emergency, car trouble or a sudden need for gas. And if that happened she would say that she herself had an emergency. Who could disprove it?

You can get away with anything if you have brass enough.

She didn't have to explain anything to this Earl, because his game was devious as her own, but they both knew she would not inquire about him from the Grovers. They both knew, too, that this was because she didn't want the Grovers to know she knew him.

He did say once, "If you should want you could leave a message. Like if those kids were coming up again."

Anne said, "Those kids will not come up again."

So far he had not pushed her to do what she knew he wanted her to do. To meet him at the cabin.

But the night did come when he pushed. August. Hot. Even up in the mountains. A lamp hung on the porch in front of Joey's, and Anne and Earl stood there for a moment. Everyone else had grumbled off. Joey stepped out and turned off the lamp. For a moment it was black as a closet. Then the big stars came out.

And then he touched her.

She sat in the Pierce Arrow, one jeweled hand resting lightly on the wheel. He put his coarse hand over hers. The warm shock of it made her blood drum.

He said, "Next time, the cabin."

She drove home with the dark wind whipping her short silken hair. There was the smell of tamaracks and then, on the flats, the smell of sage. The tires spat on the gravel.

He wanted her.

And all she had to do was to say she was going. She was Anne Patrick Lacey and she didn't have to tell anyone where she was going.

Maybe she would.

Maybe she wouldn't.

One thing had bothered her because it sounded as if he thought of her as somehow flawed. She was flawless—but how could he know? He had never seen her slim perfect feet nor her unmarked thighs.

But he had said, "Don't bring the kid."

"I can't stand the kid," he said.

23

IF YOU ASKED SPUD'S OPINION (though nobody did, except once in a while Hilary Hunter), there was trouble ahead. He had known Anne Lacey for a long time, and nothing made him more uneasy than when she perked up.

He buffed irritably at Amelia's boots. They took a nice shine. But why does a girl want to wear riding boots if she doesn't ride? Back home East, she would ride. She would ride on bridle paths with a pair of those little britches on and a round hard hat.

Back home.

He didn't know why he had lied to Amelia when he told her he had been her father's friend. He hadn't minded her father; her father was all right. But Spud had not been his friend. Yes, he did too know why he lied. He liked to keep a little bit of personal life to himself. To tell the truth, until Anne Patrick brought Will Lacey home, Spud never had laid eyes on him. That was one thing Amelia didn't know.

The other was that Spud didn't like her mother.

Never had. It was Anne's father who had been his friend.

Spud and John Patrick were born door to door in Rockland, Massachusetts, in the part known as Poverty Lane. Their mothers took tea together. Nobody on Poverty Lane expected anything. You stayed at the sisters' school as long as they would let you stay, but nobody went on to high school. Instead, you went into the shoe factory, where you might well work right beside your Da.

But for Spud's friend John Patrick, that was not enough. He went to the high school bold as Billy-be-damned, and asked the principal to give him books. At first the principal had given him a lot of poetry, but John said that wasn't what he had in mind.

After that he read math and economics and how to write a business letter, and he looked ahead and saw that people were going out more nights to hotels and restaurants, and he got a job in a business that sold kitchen equipment to hotels and restaurants and then he got a better job and then he got the business. He never had much time for Spud but he always had a buck or two for him, and after the accident—a street car hit Spud in Central Square—John Patrick came to the hospital and said when he could drive again he could drive for the Patricks because John Patrick drank, and his wife had never learned to drive.

His wife was a gentle Italian girl who did not live long enough to make much of an impression. Just before she died John Patrick bought the big house in Brookline. The front hall went up three flights; no one could keep those windows clean and the neighbors were not glad to see the Irish moving in. So when the wife died John put the child with the sisters in Newton, and Spud was the one who picked her up at the Academy on Fridays and took her back Sundays and tried to keep her busy in between. It wasn't easy. Much as he wished he liked the motherless mite, she was a hard mite to like. She wasn't loving. It wasn't so much that she was self-centered as that she didn't have any center, and the sisters said so, too.

But she was the apple of John Patrick's eye and when he knew he was going to die he asked Spud would he stick, and Spud had stuck.

Compared to Amelia—night and day. Amelia was gentle as her grandmother had been, but she worried a lot more than a girl should worry, and although Spud was glad when Hilary started coming around, it hadn't made as much difference as he'd hoped. Amelia was the real smasher, but the boys didn't seem to notice that. When she did date Hilary arranged the dates, and no fresh fellows giggled at the gate.

Hilary didn't seem to have a steady beau, but Spud had the feeling that was just because she hadn't put her mind to it. The other girls were rosy and plump and flirty the way girls ought to be. And Doll was ready.

So that—the fact that Amelia hadn't had a chance to be a flirty little kid—was one thing that Spud worried about.

Another thing. Anne liked to talk poorer than she was. So Amelia hadn't had her due. And he didn't mean boots or schools or trips. He meant that Anne was always playing poor-little-me, so her daughter was always trying to look out for poor-little-mother. A kid has the right to be a kid.

Besides, he didn't like this fellow who was snuffling around. If Anne had to have a man there were better ones. Leave out those who were married—though Spud didn't think Anne left them out just because they were married. They weren't dangerous enough. Well, this one was dangerous enough.

And if Anne ever gave him the opening, he was going to say just that. He was going to say, "Whatever this one's after, he isn't after your white body."

Maybe he wouldn't put it quite that way.

But the thing that worried him the most was that lately he kept catching Anne looking at the little one. Thoughtfully.

So sure he was sore that afternoon when Anne dropped in to see him in the only place he had ever lived in his whole life that was his. She came sashaying in in an outfit he wouldn't have been seen dead in—long floppy pants and a shirt cut down to here. She didn't beat about the bush.

She said, "I want you to move into the house."

Ever since she was a snotty little kid he had been able to see those cold wheels spinning. "Why?" he asked.

Anne said, "I need a man in the house. What if we had a fire?"

He said, "Quit your kidding."

For a moment her eyes looked just like a cat's. They widened and then blinked. She said, "I don't have to kid. Anytime I say out, you're out."

"Yes, ma'am," he said.

Briefly, their eyes threatened one another.

He couldn't figure out where she came from. Her mother had liked to make people feel good and her father had needed to be needed. Once in a while he felt sorry for her but not often, because it is hard to feel sorry for people who are sorry for themselves. Particularly if they are young and beautiful and rich.

He asked, "Who do you plan to move in here?'"

"No one," she said. "At the moment. Though it might not be a bad idea."

If it weren't for the fact that he wanted to go on living over the carriage house himself, it might not be a bad idea. But if she put anyone up there it ought to be a couple of college kids who could earn their way by doing whatever Spud told them to do. If they were nice kids, it might be good for Amelia.

The man Anne was thinking of was going to hurt somebody, though it wasn't easy to see yet who he was going to hurt. Anne and Spud could take care of themselves.

But there were some who couldn't.

"Looky here," Spud said. "Whatever that one's after —" But then because it was his tough luck to be talking to a woman, he ended lamely.

He said, "It isn't what you think he's after."

24

THAT WAS AN IMPORTANT SUMMER in Hilary's life and she had planned to use it making careful plans, but instead (though she did get as far as changing the way she wore her hair) she spent a lot of time with Kathy's parents. They interested her. They did such crazy things.

For instance, once when she dropped by she found the three of them on their knees rolling dice to see who would do the supper dishes. Now, her own parents would not do that. Sometimes they went out late at night and walked in the warm summer rains. They never minded when Hilary stayed overnight, and they read aloud.

Hilary liked it best when Kathy's mother read; she had a lovely voice. However, since the things they read were very long, it was just as well they didn't mind Hilary's staying over. They read *Pendennis* and *The Brothers Karamazov* and when they were partway through *War and Peace* Myra complained, mildly, that she didn't see much of Hilary any more.

They were like as not to have breakfast under the apple tree.

What's more, Kathy's father—who was grown—was interested in what Hilary thought.

"Why?" he would ask.

And then she would defend.

He couldn't see why she wanted to go on living in Missoula. "It isn't natural," he said. "You're supposed to want to get away."

From what? To where? You're better off where you know what you're up against. "And anyhow," she said, "you stay here."

"Ah," Kathy's father said. And he winked.

When they were reading they stopped now and then to make fudge; at those times they had some of their best fights. One of them was about Anne Lacey. They were talking about fatal beauty. Kathy's father said there wasn't any such thing. Kathy's mother said how about Greta Garbo? Hilary said how about Anne Lacey?

Kathy's father said maybe Greta Garbo. But he said, in his opinion a fatal beauty had to be capable of malevolence, and he didn't think Mrs. Lacey was smart enough for that.

Hilary said she was sure Mrs. Lacey could be malevolent if she chose.

Kathy's father asked curiously, "Why are you always sticking up for her?"

"Damn!" Kathy's mother said. "The fudge sugared again."

But the nice thing about that house was that if the fudge hadn't sugared, Hilary could have told him and told him honestly. She stuck up for Anne Lacey because the Laceys could be useful. They had the mansion and the money and even if the ladies didn't much like Anne they would accept Amelia because of the mansion and the money. And Amelia's friend. Kathy's friend, too, who had learned so much from knowing Kathy.

Like how to walk right through the library as if she belonged there, and into Kathy's father's office, where there was a reproduction of the Globe Theatre that some excited students had put together with cardboard and toothpicks. It showed the very balcony where Romeo plighted his troth to Juliet, which had turned out, Kathy's father said, much like most plighted troths.

More important: when Kathy dropped off some papers at the Kappa Kappa Gamma house, Hilary was with her. Past the pillars, it was not as grand as she had expected. The tall rooms were rather empty and the housemother surly. But she had passed the portals.

Anyhow. The first weekend in September came right after payday. Pioneer Days were over and the Chamber of Commerce had applauded those who grew beards and fined those who didn't. Rodeo, that Mardi Gras, came and went leaving the fairgrounds a shambles and headaches all over town. Kathy's folks decided that while the weather held, it would be fun to take their bottle out somewhere else. Fortunately, Hilary had her father's car.

Kathy's father had turned against cars. He had owned only one, a third-hand Ford in which the three of them had driven way out here from way back there. Oh, they had had adventures! Kathy had swollen glands in Sioux City and her father had painted her whole throat with iodine, which was not a good idea. Later, in the flat Dakotas, he drove the Ford into the barrow-pit and kept on driving there for miles before he dared to get back on the road. Local drivers were curious; one assumes they decided anything could be expected from people with Pennsylvania plates.

Just before Butte, Kathy's mother screamed and wanted to get out and walk. That was because a hundred feet below, they saw a car twisted like a child's toy and caught in the high branches of a tree. Her father said crossly that it was impossible to drive if people were going to scream, and as soon as they got to Missoula he sold the car.

Hilary knew they wouldn't like Groveland and wasn't comfortable about picnicking on the Laceys, so she suggested the site of the Girl Reserve camp. She thought it might be fun to go back there with grown-ups. How she had hated camp! You stood in line for the bad food, holding your tin plate out like Oliver Twist. The outhouse bridged a deep gully and there were flies. Hilary didn't like to make things out of leather. You had to brush your teeth in the lake. One moonlit night a fey counselor shook them out of sleep and made them dance in what she called a silver glade. She said they would never forget it. They never did.

Halfway into the second week Hilary started throwing up and had to be sent home. So much for that.

It rather pleased her to go back there older and sort of drunk. Because Kathy's father had said the girls could have one drink from his bottle, but only one because otherwise, he said, there would not be enough for him or for his wife. They all agreed.

Kathy's father was still true-blue to his bootlegger because he felt Repeal was hard on his bootlegger. You were entitled to buy from the State Liquor Stores if you were licensed (if you weren't, your friend was). But Kathy's father still went out the Rattlesnake and looked from right to left before he cheated the state and bought his booze.

He preferred that Hilary drive, and she did too. It was a nice warm sunny day and they had started early; halfway up to Hellgate they were already hungry. Kathy's mother had trouble thinking up things to eat, so Myra had packed the lunch: blueberry muffins and cold ham and hot coffee from tin cups because Myra understood that coffee is better in tin cups.

At Little Bear there were still mosquitoes and gnats and no-see-ums, which was proper. Where once she had not been permitted to swim, Hilary swam, and from the pier where she had belly flopped, she belly flopped. Kathy's parents talked to each other, which is what they often did. Much later, he wanted Hilary to sing.

"I haven't any voice," she said.

He said impatiently, "That doesn't matter."

So she sang the old songs that Myra sang. "Camptown Races" and "My Pretty Quadroon" and:

> If my beau you wants to be
> You got to have the dough and blow it on me—
> But if you ain't got no money, why you needn't come around!

All this time he took notes.

Then she sang one she loved herself, one about harps and halls that made her feel as if she wore long skirts.

> Sing me the songs that to me were so dear,
> Long, long ago. Long ago.

How long ago, do you suppose? And where had he gone after he sang those songs—around the Horn? But now all was well.

Now you have come all my grief is removed,
Let me forget that so long you have roved.
Let me believe that you love as you loved
Long, long ago. Long ago.

Then a slim sliver of a moon edged up.

But the thing that caused dissension happened on the way home.

There was this little joint with a gas pump and a neon sign, part of which worked. It was dark by then. Kathy's father said he didn't think any more whiskey, but how about a beer? The kids could probably be served if they would just put on some lipstick and act older. Hilary didn't doubt they would be served because joints don't much worry unless you're with someone of your own age. That makes a certain amount of sense.

But none of them got that cold welcome beer. Because when Kathy's mother had once looked around she pushed the girls right down the damp dark corridor into the cramped place where they didn't need to go.

Kathy said, "Why?"

"Don't sit on the seat," her mother said. She drew a careful mouth.

She said, "Because she didn't want us to see her."

And that also made sense. Because the lovely woman with the long lashes and the pale suede jacket and the cheap man was Amelia's mother.

25

No, Myra did not go back to see the doctor. What was the use?

There wasn't much anyone could do but to give it a name; the man himself as much as admitted that. It was slow. It was progressive. If an operation would help she'd be off in a flash, but an operation was not going to help. Nor would bed rest, which she would hate. Bed rest did help tuberculosis, which used to be called the White Plague. This thing that Myra had used to be called something else, too, and Myra knew what it used to be called. Her father's brother had gone the same halting way. Creeping paralysis.

The hot sun flowed like lava down the bare slopes of the hills into the basin where the Five Great Valleys meet: the Blackfoot, Mission, Hellgate, Bitterroot, and the Missoula. The hot light shimmered on the sidewalks and baked the sparse grass on the new lawns at the edge of town. Down where the Missoula River coiled the weeping willows trailed their fingers in the clear brown water. At the window of her cool dark living room Myra tightened her hands upon the sill. When Doll's mother, who was her friend, was about to die she had said, "It's too soon."

Oh yes indeed!

Yet in a way her friend had been fortunate because her departure came like a thunderclap. Then the air cleared again. The young heal. Myra would not permit the ordeal of her own young to start one moment before it had to, and meantime she would be twice as useful to everyone while she could, because she didn't want anyone to think her a nuisance.

But that is what happens, you know. No matter how much you are loved. Those who require help to move their bowels are a nuisance. Those whose faces must be swabbed down and bottoms washed. Somebody has to see that they keep something down. The halt are not fair to the firm.

So just as long as she could cope, cope she would. Not one whit of her wisdom must be lost:

> Eggs toughen if they are not cooked slowly.
> Most everyone you meet needs comforting.
> One pair—just one pair—of shoes too small
> will wreck your feet.

Never write anything down, she wrote.

Then she considered the problem of the black piano. Her sister had always wanted it; her sister could be quite cutting when she chose. But the piano had been given to Myra because she played it better, and that was because she had been willing to practice more. She had never been able to interest Hilary in the piano because Hilary had the radio and the records and Dan wouldn't have been caught dead. It was too bad, because she could have taught them just as easy. When the piano had been taken from her parents' house her sister had pressed a hankie to her eyes and then said, "Farewell, Black Beauty!"

So somewhere she had probably best write down that the piano was to go to Sister. But Sister was going to have to pay the freight. That was only fair.

Her fingers flashed and fluttered. At that time of day the living room had a nice green light. She could look up from the keys and see them all up there on the piano top: Hilary stern in her Mary Janes, Dan stern in his Buster Browns. Hank stern with his first delivery truck. It was because she was looking up at them that she struck all those discordant notes; it never in the world would have occurred otherwise.

Myra began to sing, but this time while she sang she watched her fingers closely, exacting their obedience.

I scarce knew that I was a slave,
So kind was my master to me. . . .

Nothing followed. Neither words nor melody. Just a minute, Myra Hunter, she told herself crossly. Because even if this thing was going to mean a walker and then a wheelchair and at last a bed, it was not going to involve her memory. That she would not permit. You go right back to the beginning.

. . . so gentle, so good and so brave,
I had not a wish to be free.

This time all followed where all belonged. That was more like. She was so pleased and so absorbed that she didn't hear Hank come into the room and didn't know he was about to frighten her, which he liked to do. He gripped her shoulders suddenly and kissed the nape of her neck.

"Oh, my goodness," Myra said, and she flushed right up to her curls.

"Play it again," he said, "You played it pretty."

"Oh, I don't know," she said, "it wasn't anything to write home about."

But she did play again, and this time her long plump fingers knew just where to go and what to do.

So much for that.

Hank felt that something was gathering like a storm.

He couldn't understand why he was uneasy; he had had one bad bit of news that week, but not that bad. The woman who typed out his bills for him and took his mail had quit, surprisingly, and Hank was not a man who liked to be surprised. Apparently she didn't, either. She was a nice quiet married woman who had worked for years for him and now she turned up pregnant. After she stopped being embarrassed, this woman seemed quite pleased.

Hank Hunter wasn't pleased. Over the breakfast table he looked critically at his children, who were quarreling amiably. The boy'd been speaking up to him again. Hilary could type a little and was smart as a whip, so if she was going to get hard to handle she could just watch out. She might find herself working for him after school.

He let Myra pour him coffee. She was a great comfort to him, Myra, and he unfolded the *Missoulian*. Damn it. Anyone who was fool enough to read the *Missoulian* would be uneasy. Farmers were pouring milk on the roads. Did that make any sense? Men were paid to draw on post-office walls, if they could draw. Kids from back East were clearing firebreaks in these mountains, because there wasn't a lick of work back East.

His children were well and happy. He liked his wife.

So why didn't he feel better?

For the very reason that he himself had never had it so good. No special credit to him. He had just started worrying before most others did and while they lived it up, he didn't. So here he sat with his own house in the clear, some good properties picked up cheap because of other people's troubles, and money in the bank that no one in the family knew about. When he died they were sure going to be surprised and happy.

But it isn't safe to feel safe, not with so many down on their luck. It doesn't pay. He'd seen a lot who thought they had it by the tail, and then Whatever it is that gets people got them. Besides the newspaper, Hank read *Liberty* and once in a while had a crack at *Collier's*. You had to, to keep up. But Myra read real books and often told him what she read. Once she had said that in olden days folks thought they could buy off Whatever by offering it up something or someone. Myra said Our Lord had straightened out that foolishness, but Hank was not so sure.

He decided to offer up Mr. Barry.

Well, it was more that he was going to give up some of his own comfort through Mr. Barry. Seeing Mr. Barry every day and what's more listening to him, was surely enough for anyone to offer up. But he had a job to give and Mr. Barry needed a job, so right after breakfast Hank went across the street.

The house was clean as a whistle but it smelled of ink and pencil shavings and there were too many books. Mrs. Barry was a pretty little woman, though there was not much meat on her bones.

"Oh, Mr. Hunter," she said anxiously. "I hope Jimmy hasn't done anything bad?"

That was the thin little boy. She put her hands on her son's skinny shoulders as if she were protecting him. It sort of hurt Hank's feelings. No, he had no complaint about the little fellow; in his opinion the little boy didn't do anything bad enough. Not that Hank wanted his windows broken or his lawn marked up or any kid ringing his bell and then cutting out, but it would have been more natural. If he had a little beef on him maybe he would act more natural.

Hank got right to the point. "Mr. Barry," he said, "can you type?"

Mr. Barry's brows shot up. He sat in a rat's nest of papers and with a lead pencil he kept tapping the papers.

"Certainly I type," he said. "Why do you ask?"

"Because I could use someone to do some typing."

Mr. Barry said, "Has Hilary been talking to you?"

"Why should Hilary talk to me? I'm her father." That didn't sound the way he had meant it to sound.

"The fact is," Hank said, "the woman I had typing just walked out and I thought being a teacher—I mean teachers only working part of the day and having weekends free and clear—"

"Ha!" Mr. Barry said.

If a man is nervous he will often put his hands in his pants pocket so that if they shake, no one will see. Mr. Barry thrust his hands deep into his pockets. It is possible that one might suddenly need something out of one pocket, but not two, not at the same moment unless he happened to be totally disorganized. But then, Hank suspected that Mr. Barry was. Disorganized.

To show that he himself was not nervous, Hank latched his fists to his hips and then, to keep them there, he hung his thumbs over his belt in a casual way.

"Well, there you are," he said. "I've got this job. You want it?"

In Mr. Barry's tired sallow eyes there was what Myra would have called a twinkle. He said, "I type, but I don't add well. I assume you need somebody who can add?"

Hank said, "It would help."

"Look here," Mr. Barry said. "Could you walk in and teach my classes?"

"No," Hank said honestly. "But teachers are smart. That's why they're teachers."

The somber look was back on Mr. Barry's face and Hank was glad to see it—only because he was a man who liked to see what he was used to seeing.

"But," Mr. Barry said, "I don't teach anymore."

"Yes you do too," his wife said. "In a way."

Mr. Barry looked at her with a combined affection and annoyance that made Hank feel at home. Looking past Mrs. Barry (though not in a rude way) he asked, "Why?"

Mr. Barry pointed his pencil as if he were about to lecture. "I can't do any good here anyway. Before they get to me these kids are all corrupted."

"Just a minute," Hank Hunter said.

"Don't take me wrong. They're good enough kids but they haven't been anywhere and haven't seen anything and you can't tell them anything because they don't want to know anything. As long as the sun shines and the fish jump they don't care if the country's being screwed."

It was no wonder Mr. Gilpin had to let him go. The man was a pinko and a crackpot and anyway, it was a damn funny way to talk in front of your wife.

"So the hell with it," Mr. Barry said. "I'm going where men will lay it on the line for their rights and listen when someone tells them how."

Hank said, "Where's that?"

"I guess California."

That wasn't a bad idea. For one thing, he wouldn't have the heating bills.

"Because mark my words," Mr. Barry said. "That's where the trouble's going to be."

A nut. A real nut. Who but a nut would take his wife and a nice skinny little boy to where the trouble was going to be? Hank tried to imagine traipsing off to California and dragging Myra around a lot of places she didn't want to go: rooming houses and maybe tents and wherever, no room for the piano.

And the kid. Where does a kid go to school, who does he play with? How does he explain his Dad? The pulse in his temple started to jump. That man didn't even have a car to traipse in, so they would have to traipse by bus.

Up attic there were a whole bunch of things Dan didn't use anymore: a baseball mitt, the better part of a mechanical train, ice-skates, though those wouldn't be much good in California. There was a whole first aid kit, too. Hank couldn't offer any of it.

Now it was Mr. Barry who had his hands on his boy's shoulders, and over the tousled head they looked at one another, the man who could do for his son and the man who could not. Then Mr. Barry put his hand out so that Hank had to shake it, though shaking hands is uncomfortable unless you have just met.

Mr. Barry said, "It was damn decent of you."

But it had not been enough.

But he had tried, and so perhaps he would get partial credit and be let off. Partially.

26

"I don't care," Hilary said. "I don't think it was loyal to notice."

That was nonsense and both girls knew it. That meeting had not been the sort of thing that you don't notice. So Kathy's conscience was clear about having noticed, but it was not so clear about having told Janet because Janet never could keep her mouth shut. Being defensive, Kathy got angry, the way one does.

"Why shouldn't she?" she asked. "She has a perfect right."

But if Anne Lacey were seen about with the wrong men it would damage what had become her precarious place in Missoula. And that would damage Amelia's place and that, in turn, would do no good for Hilary who was Amelia's friend.

"People will talk," she said stiffly.

Kathy said, "You know, Missoula isn't the whole wide world."

Hilary had stopped torturing her hair; it hung now like a fall of silk. Her carefully darkened eyebrows rose. She wasn't going to comment on anything as silly as that.

"Besides, how do you know that man's the wrong sort?"

"Well, I've got eyes. And anyhow, unless, he wouldn't take her to a place like that. Nobody goes to places like that but trash."

Kathy said, "We were there."

That wasn't the same thing at all. They were there for a lark. Anne was clandestine.

"I'm not sure you can use the word that way," Kathy said.

Hilary said, "I think you'll find you can."

A chill fell between them.

They were sitting in the bright fall sunshine on the steps of Main Hall, which was Hilary's favorite of all places. It was still almost as warm as summer and in front of them the carpet of the Oval was still green, but there was a difference in the air, a quickness and bustle, and though on the trees the leaves were dusty green, one dry leaf suddenly scuttled at their feet with a tap like a blind man's cane.

They were there because Kathy claimed to need a book she couldn't find at the Public Library. That was a big stony building with dim stacks but a nice children's room, with those low round tables just big enough for Baby Bear. To this day Hilary was wistful about those tables, which she had liked very much. You could twist your feet around the legs of the chairs and rest your elbows on the pleasant table tops; the children who sat there were not even old enough to deface them.

The steps of Main Hall were not as comfortable but Hilary liked them because many people went up and down and saw her sitting there, perfectly at ease on campus. Even if they didn't know her name, this time next year they would know her name, you bet.

Kathy never knew when to leave well enough alone. She spoke again of Mrs. Lacey.

"I thought you admired her," Kathy said.

"I did," Hilary told her.

"My father thinks she's very sexy," Kathy said.

"I suppose she is," Hilary said in the clear cold voice of one to whom sex is not that interesting.

She pushed back her foxy hair. She wondered which would shock her mother most—that a grown man should use that word before his daughter, or that her own daughter should relinquish a friend. Because Anne Lacey had been a friend of sorts and had taught Hilary how to get in and out of rooms and how not to outstay one's welcome. And Hilary had indeed defended Anne hotly against her mother's mild criticisms. Well, she had been younger then.

However, Myra's reactions were not easy to predict. Hilary and Doll, against their better judgment, had taken her to see *The Good Earth*. They thought she would detest the concubine. Instead, she spoke right up for her. The girl had not been faithful, but what could you expect? When she had nothing to do all day but get dolled up and loll around with that old banjo.

She said, "Your father wouldn't put up with it."

At the notion of Myra all dolled up and lolling around, the girls muffled their laughter in their fists.

Now Kathy said, suspicious, "What's so funny?"

Hilary only said, "Tell you sometime."

Because that was a day of shocks. That very instant she had become aware that in the eyes of some, Kathy was sexy.

For some minutes Hilary's attention had been idly engaged by a young man, one very much like all the other young men except that this one was taller than most, more somber, and atypical. He was alone. Mostly, if they were not at the moment paired with a young woman, the young men traveled in groups, as if they thought that was safer. They were probably right. This one was seated on a slatted bench and looking at them. Correction: he had been looking at Kathy.

And, treacherously, Kathy knew it, too. She sat very straight. She crossed her legs so that from beneath her rather longish skirt one foot hung gracefully; she held her chin high and when she spoke she turned in such a way that the watcher watched. The treachery lay not so much in the fact that Kathy knew someone was watching her, but that she had in no way indicated that fact to her friend.

Many, many things are more important than young men; Hilary had thought that about this she and Kathy were in accord. Each would require—and obtain—one later. Meantime, she had observed that except nominally, there is no friendship between women once one has found a man, since one becomes distracted and the other critical. Who needs a man?

This young man arose. He walked to the one tree that had flung a yellow flag to the indifferent sky and, in defiance of the Board of Regents and the entire state of Montana, he plucked it. He did. He broke the branch right off. He damaged the tree. Then he walked straight to Kathy and placed it across her knees.

"This is for you," he said.

And then he went away.

Kathy's cheeks turned red as a sugar maple, although in Montana there are no sugar maples.

"All right," Hilary said. "Who's he?"

She thought her friend would be evasive. Not at all.

"My father's best student," Kathy said. She met Hilary's gaze straight on. "He's a senior."

A senior! That was another generation.

"He is very poor," Kathy said. "And very proud." She rose, holding the branch like a bouquet. "We may as well start home," she said.

Of course. Since the young man had come and gone. Hilary picked up the book that had been the purpose of their being here.

She said, "Here. This is what we came for. Isn't it?"

One of those mean little winds that come with the start of the first semester slid through the Hellgate. A second leaf moved crabwise to huddle by the first. Both girls shrugged into the cardigans of their twin-sweater sets.

"If he's so smart," Hilary said, "how come what a funny thing to do?"

"Because that's what they read this week. *The Golden Bough.*"

"Just the same," Hilary said.

"Oh," Kathy said modestly, "he doesn't pay any attention to rules and things like that."

Before they got to where they were going to part, they had to go by the Lacey block. It always looked cold, no matter what the season. Behind the tall iron fence the blue spruce perpetually wept damp needles. Nothing moved. Above, the shingled turrets frowned through their shuttered lids. Kathy said, "I suppose we ought to stop?"

Hilary thought about it. Then she said, "No. My mother's looking for me."

That wasn't true. It would have been more accurate to say that Hilary was looking for her mother. You think you have everything straightened out and then you don't. You think you know everything about everyone and then you find out you don't know much about anyone at all. By and large, Myra didn't change.

There was one thing, however, that Hilary wanted to straighten out and thought that on the whole, she could. Apparently, the way things were working out, Amelia wasn't going to be much help to Hilary. That didn't mean that Hilary didn't have to help Amelia.

So she said, "There's one thing I want understood."

Kathy said, "I know what you want understood."

And so for the moment, that friendship lasted.

For that moment Hilary thought that they both knew what they were talking about. She meant she was going to raise merry hell if Kathy ever opened her mouth. What Kathy meant was how wonderful he was.

Kathy said, "And he likes my father. Though he may have to shoot him."

Whyever why?

Kathy explained. After the revolution, there wouldn't be any place for her father.

Even Mr. Barry never talked like that. Hilary didn't for a moment think that Kathy thought anyone might shoot her father, but she was offended that Kathy joked about it. Even for fun, she herself would not shoot her father. Would they lead him, perhaps, to his own fence, where his petunias were? Would they cover his eyes? Well, if anyone tried to shoot Hank Hunter, they would get what-for. She, Hilary, would see to it.

She asked, "Are there other nuts like that around?"

"Oh yes indeed," Kathy told her. "They're all over. Mrs. Roosevelt goes around and talks to them."

Then carefully carrying her branch, Kathy turned homeward. For a moment Hilary stood, reflecting. No, she would not like it one bit if someone shot her father. She liked her mother, too. Exhilarating as it was to be grown, it had been very nice to be small, too. Good things had happened. Like measles.

When Hilary and Dan had measles at the same time and Myra was almost out of her wits, she put them both together in her big bed. When she had read them everything they didn't want to hear and while they itched and scratched and were so hot and could smell their own fever, then Myra said, "Oh, hush."

And then she sang.

Dan was on one of her billowy sides and Hilary on the other; the room got cool and darker.

> Father will come to his babe in the nest,
> Silver sails all out of the west . . .

Do you know what happened? Father came.

27

DOLL WAS THE LAST PERSON to know that she was going steady.

Her brother didn't mind Con and her father sort of liked him. "If you ask me," her father said, "he's a whole lot better than some of those pipsqueaks who used to hang around."

It gave Doll quite a turn, because come to think of it, it had been quite a time since a pipsqueak had hung around. Word gets about and she hadn't even noticed.

For one thing, she'd been awfully busy since school took up again. Although there wasn't any question of her going on after, she did want to graduate High. It seemed to her that there was something low-down and licked about not graduating High. And it wasn't as easy for Doll as for some, so she couldn't help being glad that Janet was having trouble, too. Janet had put off geometry as long as possible and now she had to pass. Her father threatened her with a tutor.

Doll's trouble was more diffuse, though so far, she had managed to squeak by. Her teachers liked her and encouraged her, they—so to speak—whistled and patted their knees to keep her trying. Everyone knew she had a whole lot to do at home. This year her name came up at the first faculty meeting. Teachers are not unkind. The problem was to find five courses Doll could pass.

Mrs. Grey, who looked like a tiny Arthur Rackham drawing, as if she grew oddly and gently out of a gnarled tree, said "I cannot teach this girl Latin."

Everyone was afraid of Mrs. Grey; she had connections with the University and had published. For a small woman, she was formidable.

"But I do not see," she continued in her weak, severe voice, "why this dear warm hard-working girl needs languages."

Oh, they agreed! However, she did need five courses.

Mrs. Wincke said chemistry was out. But General Science was not hard and it never hurt anyone to know where to put a well that would not be contaminated. Because you never know.

Young Mr. Winston who was new that year rushed to the office and came back with the glad news that Doll had not had American History, which anyone could pass. This offended the man who taught American History.

The pretty lady with a long pink nose who could not keep discipline and cried in her office said she could not teach Doll French. She would be happy to try, she said, but she just knew she couldn't, and her blue eyes filled with tears, which made everyone feel responsible and glad (later) when she married and didn't have to think about anything again.

Then a handsome woman who taught Drama and Public Speaking and was crippled said she had had Doll once in public speaking and it had not turned out very well. However, she was planning to do Capek—Doll would do nicely as a robot; after that she could work on makeup and properties.

That made three. Two to go.

The man who had replaced Mr. Barry said that in his opinion there were no right or wrong answers you could give in Problems of American Democracy and Doll could pass if she would just show up. Four.

Then little Miss Finklestein for the first time in three years spoke up. She also turned bright red. It is not easy to speak up—you may offend. Besides, since she taught typing she was not a real teacher. But if it is a moral matter, one must speak.

So she said in a voice so firm that young Mr. Winston turned and looked at her with interest, "This girl types very well. I realize that she cannot repeat my course without first having failed it, but if the principal approves I could, perhaps, initiate an advanced course in secretarial skills." Then she said primly, "Naturally, any qualified student could elect this course."

Five!

They parted glowing with good will.

Particularly, Miss Finklestein glowed. Not only had she not offended, but as they tried to pass together through the door, young Mr. Winston asked if she would care to have supper with him? At the Coffee Pot?

Everything changed.

The girls no longer took their jelly sandwiches to Doll's house at noon. That was because Doll was no longer there at noon. Since Con could only date on Sundays, she brought her lunch in a paper bag and so did he, and they ate in his truck. She was always watching fearfully for signs that he was like the others and might want to go to her house while her father and brother were not there.

He had not once suggested it.

Doll had not yet met his father, though Con had demanded early to meet hers. Sunday afternoons she brought the picnic, or if it rained they went to the movies, which cost him cold cash.

Then in late fall, Indian summer fell upon a Sunday.

All week Doll had been getting out winter clothes and hanging them upon the line to rid them of the smell of mothballs. She had brought in the overshoes from their summer position and located the knitted caps and the earmuffs. This Sunday, it was hot! The air was hazy, the sun coppery. Doll hummed as she put their lunch together.

She wore California pants and sneakers that laced up her ankles; Con said they might do some hiking. The kitchen steamed from the roast and Doll had splashed cold water on her forehead and her wrists, but just the same she took her old striped jacket that looked as if it had been made of blankets. Everyone knows a coppery sun and a hot haze doesn't mean that by nightfall sly winds may not sneak down like coyotes: in the morning there may be a skiff of snow.

They headed toward Grass Valley and Con said, "First, we will stop so you can meet my Dad."

She could not imagine why her heart started racketing, because she was not a shy person, or not that shy. Perhaps it was because Con sounded very stern indeed, and while sometimes she liked that, sometimes she didn't. You can see how that would be. Why, they had been past that house a dozen times, and he had never said!

It was everything she had always hoped to avoid. Though nothing sagged and nothing leaned, the house needed paint and in the sunny silence Doll could hear chickens cackling out in back. Expectable and unsightly machines stood about. A buck-rake and a sulky-rake. A grindstone with a gas-driven engine for sharpening scythes and saws. There was a certain amount of order within this disorder—nothing was rusted nor broken and there were no corpses of old cars. Over all the tall gaunt frame of a beaver-slide brooded. The huge barn had a sod roof upon which grasses blew, so it must have been there for a long time; nobody builds barns like that anymore.

Con said, "They say when the barn's bigger than the house, you know who wears the pants."

Doll frowned. It was clear to her who meant to wear the pants.

In a pasture beside the barn two handsome horses moved. "The bay's my Dad's," Con said. "The gray's mine. This way."

They went in through the back, which was fitting. Nobody wants mud and dust and bits of straw tracked in through the front. The kitchen, where the father expected them, was a big brown room with cracked linoleum and a clean braided rug. The long table was big enough to seat a hay-crew, and you knew whose job that would be. Doll saw that although the big room was sunk in tarnished light (a coat of paint would help) the windows were tall and the sills wide enough for begonias.

She was surprised to see a glistening enamel gas stove, for which the blackened wood range had not been displaced. Nobody would replace a good wood range. What would you do in winter?

Con saw her eye upon the stove and said, "Dad and me like to be comfortable. Next year we're going to get a Kelvinator. This is Dad."

His Dad sat at the table with a newspaper spread out and on the newspaper a great many parts of something complicated. He had a gentle smile and a countryman's seamed face and very little conversation.

"Pleased to meet any friend of Con's," was the way he put it.

He was not young, but probably not as old as he had weathered.

"My Dad knows cattle," Con said. "Someday we're going to show them."

His Dad smiled, pleased. He said, "Con's got some big ideas," and then as if he were afraid he might have said something hurtful, "not that there's nothing wrong with big ideas."

When they left Doll said she was very glad to have met him.

"Similar," he said. He sounded as if he meant it, too.

Outside again, Con sighed as if they had just undergone something dangerous but necessary. Pointing up to a blue distant hill he said, "That's where we're going to hike."

"Oh," she said.

"Unless," he said, "you'd rather ride? Our horses don't take much to strangers."

Doll did not take much to horses.

"It's not as far as it looks," he said. "Not really."

Up they went.

Going up is not so steep as coming down and Con had a knapsack, so he didn't have to carry anything. The worst part was quite near the beginning, when they passed a big old bull with curved wicked horns.

"You don't have to worry about Hereford bulls," Con told her. "Watch out for the cows. Guernseys, it's just the other way, but then," he added practically, "who wants Guernseys?"

Up there, the shade was deep. From their feet the land tumbled down to the plush floor of Grass Valley, where his father's house and barn and bunkhouse and sheds were scattered like jacks.

"Look there," Con said.

He meant the big field with the fenced haystacks, where tiny cattle didn't seem to move.

Con said, "Those are ours. Seventy-eight cows and steers."

Doll wasn't sure whether this was a lot or not enough.

"My," she said.

Beside them a narrow stream caught its breath, shouted downward and then, subdued, wandered through hay-land to the Bitterroot.

"This here's called Bloody Dick," Con said. "We got the water rights. You don't say much."

She said, "I was just thinking."

Once she had read a book. She had to. She didn't remember a whole lot about the book except the picture in the front of it. A small girl sat and what you saw was what she was seeing— the great frozen waterfall of the Alps. Snow on the purple peaks. Blue forests. Far below, the small roof of a home.

She said, "It's pretty."

He said, "Oh, God, yes."

After a while he said, "Let's eat."

Presently they lay back upon the thin old Army blanket and watched through the dark branches the white clouds, slowly swimming the deep sea of the sky.

Con said, "My Dad got through 1919. He'll pull through this one too."

"Oh, sure," Doll said.

"There's a lot of sage flats down there, although you may not think. I'm going to buy it up and grub sage and irrigate. And then," he said, "I will run a thousand head. Do you understand?"

"No," Doll said. "Want a pickle?"

"And then," Con said dreamily, "I'll build a big house with bathrooms everywhere. My wife will have help in the kitchen and fur coats. And when I walk into the bank they're going to say—you know what they're going to say?"

How could she?

"Here comes the King of Grass Valley."

She wanted to reach out and touch the rough black hair. The hurt she felt for him was sudden as a stubbed toe. Oh, one should never, never aim too high. If what you set your heart on is a small apartment, maybe even up over a store, and matching dishes—you may get it. But bathrooms everywhere!

And then Con said a strange fierce thing. He said, "My old man's going to live with me till the last day he lives."

"Goodness," she said. "This was supposed to be a picnic."

The shadows suddenly shot forward. There was still sunlight on the slopes but down below the valley brimmed with dusk.

"I'd better get you back," he said.

But first, before he got her back, he put the hard palm of his hand against her palm. He smelled of sweet clean human sweat.

"You understand," he said, "this isn't overnight. For quite a while, she'd have to put up."

Put up with the muddied yard, the scrabbling hens, the greasy separator? The once in a while trip to town? Put up with the hay-crew silently wolfing their way through the dog days? Below, the dusk took the little cattle, the buck-rake, the gaunt beaver-slide. The high wheel of the wind-charger winked and went out.

He said, "Would you put up?"

Whoever put up would put up till the last day she lived. The children would have to go to school in work shoes. The barn would always be bigger than the house.

"Would you?" he asked. "Would you put up?"

She took her hand away from his.

"Oh yes," she said. "I will."

28

THE FIRST TIME the thought skittered into Anne's mind it was unsubstantial as a gray leaf scraping cement, or as a mouse.

What if something should happen to the child?

Of course she didn't want anything to happen to the child. She was the child's mother.

But what if?

Once she had pocketed her pride and gone to Warm Springs, where the state hospital was, so that the doctors there could tell her what she could expect. They said there was nothing that she could expect. They took her through the wards so she could see there were some worse off than she. The smell of the wards seeped out into the halls. She saw children who drooled and could not be toilet trained—these were retarded. She saw children whose white faces were still and cold except when their eyes blazed—these were mad. They were all mixed together, with here and there a few strapped to their cribs.

"We're understaffed," the doctors said. "There's no money."

For some time afterward she got letters asking if she could help. She sent checks once or twice, but she didn't like to have those letters coming to her plainly marked on the official stationery of such a place. Eventually they stopped.

They had also told her that the severely retarded often do not live beyond fifteen or so. No one knew why. They simply got to fifteen or so and then stopped living.

Fifteen was forever.

In the meantime it was hard on her because Earl resented the child very much. He had no pride; he didn't mind that Anne paid for everything. But he would not move into the carriage house. It would have been so much easier. She would let it be known that Spud was too old and there were things around that needed doing. She couldn't very well call him the chauffeur because nobody in Missoula had chauffeurs and everyone knew she liked to drive. It was nobody's business anyway, and if he worked for her she could fire him anytime.

He would have done it, too, if it were not for the child. Anne did not understand why he minded to the extent he minded. It was irrational, but the irrational have great power. You can't out-guess them: How do you know what they are going to do when they don't know themselves?

"Why do you mind so much?" Anne asked him. "Is there some special reason?"

"Don't ever talk like that to me," he said.

"All right," Anne said.

She knew what Spud thought Earl was after. But challenging him amused her and she would pay his way as long as he amused. It's more fun to have the whip hand if the other person also has a whip. The challenge came in seeing how far she could go. She had to watch those pale eyes and remember that in spite of their sexual collisions, he could turn on her anytime. Or leave her.

Lately he had been talking about California.

"What's around here for me?" he asked.

"For one thing," she had answered, "you don't have to do very much."

He said, "I wouldn't do very much in California."

"Don't you like the lake?" They both knew she wasn't talking about the lake.

He shrugged. He said, "It's all right. It's getting cold up there."

She said, "Feel free to go."

He said, "You bet your boots I will."

So that was another reason for the carriage house. Of course he couldn't stay at the lake all winter. Already, he had quit work-ing for the Grovers. What made Mrs. Grover mad was that he walked off the job without helping them close up. What made Anne mad was that Mrs. Grover had the nerve to call Anne Lacey to know where he was at.

However should she know?

Mrs. Grover laughed. "I guess we all know it won't be your pump that freezes," was what she said.

Anne was about to charge Earl with having been indiscreet, and then she thought she wouldn't. It might be more useful at some later time and meantime, it was an Ace in the Hole. Spud himself had taught her poker, and if Earl thought that in any sense she was going to give anything away, he had another think coming. The version of the game she preferred was Dealer's Choice.

But lately Earl had been bored and sullen. Just this last week he had said, "Look. You won't marry me and I know why, but can't we both go to California?"

She said, "On my money?"

But this time he wasn't kidding around. He was about fed up. She could tell.

It was right after that that her migraines began again.

Amelia worried, which annoyed her. "I'm perfectly all right," Anne said. "Do you think you could just leave me alone?"

She slept a great deal. Everyone learned to tippy-toe. Sometimes whole afternoons went by.

Finally she said, "What's your little friend's name?"

She was talking about Janet, and the reason she wanted to know was that she didn't choose to go back to the old doctor who had brought her children and buried her husband and had never liked her.

The new young doctor might be more receptive. He waited until she had buttoned up and then he said, "What's your real problem?"

She dropped her lashes and then lifted them suddenly and gave him a long open look. It always got them.

She said, "I can't sleep."

Because he was a gentleman he didn't wink, but he might, just as well have. He was not a bad-looking man at all and closer to her own class. Idly, she wondered if he would be any fun. Probably not, because doctors on the whole are self-protective. He was tall and had lots of brown wavy hair; maybe he was a little loose around the middle.

She said, "Do you play golf?"

"Every weekend," he said.

No. It wouldn't do. Anne supposed that she could get him if she wanted him, but if she got him, she would have to keep him. Doctors can afford one clean-cut divorce and one new start, but they cannot afford whispering. Nobody trusts a man capable of illegal passion; his practice would fall away. If he divorced his wife there would have to be some kind of settlement. Six months later everyone would be tired of talking about it, but every weekend he would still play golf, and Anne would be the wife who had to sit around the pool at the Country Club with all the other women, waiting until it was late enough to drink.

No thank you.

"All I want," she said, "is something to help me sleep."

Then because men are easily confused and it is usually best to confuse them, she opened her eyes wide again to their gray depths.

"I am not suicidal," she said.

"No," he said. "I don't believe you are."

So he gave her the piece of white paper with the chicken scratches on it. No one can read those scratches. Many a one has wondered if the doctor calls the druggist before you get there, to make all clear. Anne took the small pills home and gratefully tucked them away, although she didn't know why she wanted them.

But maybe someday they would come in handy.

Then in November Earl said she could do what she liked. He was leaving, with her or without. If she had changed her mind and wanted to come along, he wouldn't mind.

She thought of the soft skies and the blue surf. Why shouldn't she spend some money? It was hers. She could rent something nice and they could live in it as man and wife. If it weren't for the child. But perhaps for a nice place to live and a fast car and cash in his pocket . . . ?

She said, "I'd have to bring the child."

"Nix," he said.

She didn't believe him in November, but before Christmastime, he left.

He sent her a postcard from a very grand hotel where she knew that he wasn't staying. The card showed the azure pool and it showed the white beach. "Wish you were here," was the way the message went. "Ha-ha!" The return address, which was not the address of the hotel, was very carefully printed.

In January the child came down with the flu and ran a high temperature. However, she recovered.

"Mother," Amelia kept saying, "can I get you anything?"

February.

Damage her own child? Are you crazy?

He wasn't as attractive as her own perversity may have encouraged him to think. There were not many wealthy women who would take up with someone who, publicly, would do them so little credit. She let enough time go by to let him worry, and then she tried the carefully printed address. Of course it might be a *false* false address, but she didn't think so. It might be the address of an acquaintance or of someone he had simply paid in order to pick up his mail, but she was pretty sure that what she mailed, he would pick up.

He wasn't that through with her yet. Nor she with him. What Earl had done was dishonest, even if it was not illegal. Because she had bought him, and he had turned around and taken her property to California. Facts are facts. He had run out on a contract, and when she got him back he was going to pay for it.

When she wrote to him she was cautious, as suspicious people are. She used Amelia's typewriter, even for her signature, so that if for any reason she should ever wish to deny having written it, she could. Then she drove to Stevensville and mailed the envelope from there so that it wouldn't have the Missoula postmark.

What she wrote was deliberately businesslike. "I find I again require a caretaker for my cabin at Little Bear Lake, which should be opened by the first of May. At the very latest. I shall discuss remuneration only if you are interested."

She was not at all sure he knew what remuneration meant, but if he didn't, she was sure he would find out.

Then she began to wait.

29

Myra was gleeful as a child. No one had noticed! Women often complain that no one notices, and sometimes men complain about it too, but on the whole you are lucky if no one notices.

But as the thick winter days thinned into February Myra began to jot more wisdom down. Just in case. And because it was not as easy as it used to be to get the hatbox down, she collected bits of paper on which she had noted interesting and useful thoughts. These she tucked into pockets and behind the pepper mill. She usually remembered the ones behind the pepper mill, but pockets are harder because they do go into the wash, and once or twice when she got to the ironing, a sage thought had gone. Wisdom should not go through the wash.

Maxims of Myra:

> If you have to think about it, don't.
> Don't be bossy, because people don't like it, and
> if you try to boss them they will sneak.

She frankly and honestly believed that that was true. And that reminded her that

> Never say anything about anyone, including you.

There is much too much talk. Oh, Hilary, oh, Dan. There is so much harm done by talk. My goodness, if anybody knew how many times she had been furious! And with good reason! So:

> Keep your fury to yourself.

You didn't mean it really, did you? And besides, you don't want to be remembered as one who was furious.

Then there were times, when she had changed her apron, when she got mysterious messages back. One, which was badly blurred, said:

Change.

Whatever had she meant?

Had she meant that one should be flexible? Because that is a great help. If you are wrong, you had better be able to stop being wrong. But since she was not sure that anyone was wrong, she added a question mark.

Sometimes in the night she woke frightened. Then, being a reasonable woman, she thought (while Hank moved slightly in his sleep) *We all face this.*

He giveth with the one hand and with the other He takes away. But He giveth.

Myra had always been a selfish woman. She always had wanted to be the first to go.

Right in the middle of the damp, drab year there comes a day when a chinook moves down from Canada trailing warm robes of wind. The snow melts. Rivulets run down the mountain sides; in the gutters brown water glitters. People open their coats, the sun is hot on their foreheads. There is a great deal of strolling around. There are not many pigeons in Missoula, but Hilary saw one in Greenough Park, preening its Joseph's throat.

Kathy and Hilary could not afford to waste a chinook, and they cut school.

They could afford to. Both of them were passing. And suppose you missed one day? Winter would howl again tomorrow.

Greenough Park was pleasant, not very big but singularly uncluttered. The young did not frequent this park: why should they, with the whole Rocky Mountains all around? The park was small but had been given to the town: one of the Greenoughs had married a Boissevain, one of the Boissevains had married Edna St. Vincent Millay. It wasn't a very close connection, but close enough so that it was where Kathy and Hilary liked to come.

> Your face is like a kingdom where a king
> Dies of his wounds, untended and alone. . . .

Oh, they would tend him!

The sun struck through the bare architecture of the trees and the melted puddles struck right back. The benches were very damp. Eventually the shadows moved and so did the girls. The poet's silver hair, her tragic eyes, oh—she was beautiful—moved them as much as they always had.

> The wind of their endurance, driving south,
> Flattens your words against your speaking mouth. . . .

Someday they too would find a dying king.

But right now, since no king was in sight, it was closer to home by the Van Buren Bridge. On that side of town many poor students bed-and-boarded because on that side it was cheaper. You could walk to campus. But at the Van Buren Bridge, Hilary met a curious king. Why, she had not meant to meet anyone like that for years and years and if she did, she had not meant to meet this one.

But what happened was that right on that old bridge they ran into the young man of the golden branch, and he had a friend. In these circumstances there is a certain protocol. You drop back so that your friend may walk with whom she wishes to walk with.

His friend was tall and tragic. Perhaps it was just his heavy brows, but he did look as if he were thinking. His shoulders were very broad and his hips narrow. Hilary knew that Myra would say this didn't make any difference, but it does. If a man's hips are broad, you cannot take him seriously.

He asked Hilary what she was majoring in, which assumed that she was old enough to be majoring.

> I remember an ugly coat you wore
> Plaided black and white. . . .

It was not so much that his coat was ugly—but it was too short in the sleeves and it was frayed.

She had not been brought up to lie and so she said only that she was interested in literature.

He nodded glumly.

She countered quickly. "And your major?"

Do you know what he said? He said theology.

Nobody majors in theology.

Then he said truthfully, "That's not true."

Both of them were carefully not looking at the others.

"There's no theology major," he said. "Here."

They stopped for a moment on the bridge, where the February water swirled below: it plaited and braided and sucked at the banks, and vomited bad things. One bad thing was a small animal. Its backbone showed where whatever was meant to gnaw on it had gnawed it. Hilary was a tall girl, but this tall young man looked down on her.

"*Memento mori*," he said. "*Dominus vobiscum.*"

Heavens. Perhaps he was a Roman Catholic? There were a lot of them over around Butte.

Behind his gold spectacles his eyes flashed like the sunstruck puddles. "From here," he said, "I'm going to Yale."

Nobody goes to Yale. Yale is back East and for the sort of person who drives Cords and goes to New York City just to lark around.

Myra had said there are things that you may ask as long as you ask courteously, so as courteously as such a question can be asked, she asked, "Can you afford?"

He flushed, and as if he confessed to some shocking habit he said, "I have a fellowship."

That gave her something to think about.

Though she had never heard of fellowships. Kathy would know.

But after that it was hard to get Kathy's attention, because she was tossing her hair about and sort of dancing. It was so obvious that she wished to be asked that Hilary did the friendly thing and asked.

She said, "So?"

"He asked me out. He did, he asked me out!"

Hilary said practically, "Will they let you?"

"Whyever not?"

Because he was too old, that was whyever not. On the other hand, people of your own age are not all that safe.

Kathy said, "Come home with me?"

Kathy's mother would probably make raisin bread toast. But if Hilary went home with Kathy she would have to call home, and Myra wouldn't mind about the raisin bread but she was quick to catch guilt, and Hilary had cut school.

"I guess not," she said. "Not today."

What else?

That same day Janet's father ratted on Myra. Doctor or not, like his daughter, he talked too much. The apple does not fall far from the tree. That afternoon Hank Hunter had been delivering coal. The doctor, with his hands on his hips, watched to see that he got every scuttle's worth. He got every scuttle's worth.

Assured of that, he asked, "Why didn't your wife come back?"

Naturally Hank was startled. He had seen his wife this very morning at breakfast. They had flapjacks.

The doctor told him in detail what the trouble was but Hank did not require the details because he remembered Myra's uncle. Do you know terror? Your blood escapes your veins.

This doctor said, "It isn't going to happen all at once."

Thank God.

"You haven't noticed?"

Yes, he had noticed. He just hadn't wanted to notice. Here is this good person who suddenly drops things: she who had always been so careful. Walks with one hand against the wall. Of course he had noticed. The first thing he thought was that he had to talk to Dan, who was the other man. Or Hilary, who was the other woman. But he knew that they couldn't help; they could only be hurt before they needed to be hurt.

"If I see she gets back to you," he said, "what can you do?"

"Well, to be honest," the doctor said, "not very much. To be honest."

"Then why get back to you?"

"Tests. Therapy. Keep her a bit more comfortable."

Hank said, "The Mayo Clinic? Salt Lake City?"

"No," the doctor said.

It can't be much fun to have to tell bad news, not unless you are naturally mean. This fellow did not seem naturally mean. He said, "No one knows anything. Will you bring her in?"

No.

Not if they could only try to make her comfortable. No. Her husband would make her comfortable and he would do it by letting her fool him. Just as long as possible and then for a while.

He told the doctor. He said, "I guess not."

30

Fortunately Anne heard the mailbox tick and then the mailman's steps, retreating.

The damn fool had scrawled on a penny postcard for all the world to see. From Earl's point of view, that was okay. But don't tell her that people in post offices do not read postcards, because they do.

She knew he wouldn't make out in California. He was not about to pick grapes. So she wore a small smile at the beginning of his message. So far she was not in any way personally involved. Then the smile vanished. "Just don't ever let me see the kid."

The wicked have no vices. They cannot afford them. Anne Lacey had no room for drink, drugs, or love. She had no room, either, for the inadequate child.

It posed a pretty problem. Warm Springs was out. She understood that some who could afford to paid vast sums to keep the handicapped out of sight. Well, she was not going to pay vast sums, not with cattle prices the way they were and no end in sight. So what was she going to do about Earl?

She was not in love with him—she would have been offended at the suggestion—but he had brought a lot of fun and anger into her life. No, it was not a love affair but a battle: perhaps an Indian skirmish. The question was who was going to win. She meant to. Her body had a certain place in her arsenal, but since she herself was not much interested in bodies, she was not deluded. Her best weapon was the First National Bank.

His best was his aversion to her child.

There came a day in March when she had one of her migraines. You cannot plan a migraine, and unless other necessary

coincidences occur, there is no sense in having one. On this particular day—it was a Wednesday—the wind wept. Rain hurled
beneath the shingles and worried one of them away. Anne
watched it sail. Even if Spud had been at home, he could not be
expected to climb up there. But Spud was not at home. The cold
wet weather twisted his bad leg and he had gone downtown to the
outpatients' at St. Patrick's, where you had to wait your turn but
didn't pay as much, and he had told Anne belligerently that after
that he was going right up to his room and go to bed.

Mrs. Phelps called to say her niece needed her.

Why, that meant Anne was left all by herself with not a soul
to help! Of course her migraine struck.

The child was troublesome. She kept hiding. She did that
often, but Mrs. Phelps always knew where to look and Spud
usually had a pretty good idea. Today she hid beneath the dining room table. Mrs. Phelps kept a linen cloth on that table and
because the cloths had all belonged to the old people they were
damask and hung to the floor like gorgeous tents. Anne herself
could see why that might be nice. It was a secret place, but light.

She herself would not have hidden in the pantry. When she
heard the child scurrying there she didn't even bother to open
the door to look. Mrs. Phelps kept the Lysol out of reach, and
the ammonia.

The game was too macabre for a woman with a pounding
head. She locked the child in her bedroom and the child screamed
until she let her out again. It was too much. It was much too much.

Since the child could not tell time, Anne tried to give her lun-
cheon early, but she would not eat. Anne knew this was because
she preferred Mrs. Phelps to feed her, but she took it as a personal
slight. What was so grand about Mrs. Phelps? The child did not
want the soup nor the Jell-O nor any part of the banana.

It honestly looked to Anne as if the cold rain might let up.
She stood by the living room window and looked out. Yesterday
the snow had melted some but today the raw wind froze the top
again. You would plunge through the rime and into the cold slush.

The wind nibbled the eaves. She closed her eyes and leaned her forehead against the icy glass. There were a score of places in the old house where a child could hide if a child wanted to frighten and confuse.

In a way she could understand Earl.

Amelia had been a quiet youngster and adept at entertaining herself. She read early and easily. You always knew where she was. She was either on the window seat with a book or magazine— *John Martin's Book*, that magazine was called. Amelia liked *Peter Puzzlemaker*. Or she was in her room endlessly rearranging the furniture in her doll's house. The pink and blue metal furniture was by Tootsietoy. The chiffonier had a real mirror. Then she went off to first grade and nobody had to think about her anymore.

While Anne just stood there by the window, the child hid in the deep hall closet. This time Anne thought: all right. Let her. But she couldn't just let the child lurk in there because if anyone came in—perhaps Mrs. Phelps, released from her emergency—it would look odd.

She said, "I see you. I see you in there."

What Anne saw was not the child, but the hangers in the closet swinging. But if Anne had seen the child, she knew its eyes would shine like a small animal's. Not a dangerous one, but one of the quick, startling scary kind.

What in the name of God was Anne Patrick Lacey doing here in the hallway on her hands and knees, trying to entice an idiot from a closet floor? By now her head felt as if it were alternately swelling and shrinking. No one has to put up with that.

"Darling," she said, and the child trembled in her arms.

"Why, darling," she said again.

And then ever so sweetly, Anne dressed the child.

She put her little snowsuit on and her little hat with the ear-muffs and the little red rubber boots, and she did not forget the mittens nor the scarf.

Then she opened the door of the old Lacey mansion and put the child out.

"Sister will be home by and by," she said gently. "Sister will give you lunch."

And then she went upstairs and took her sleeping pills—not all of them; just enough.

When Amelia found her the little girl was crouched in the deep end of the swimming pool, presumably because the pool was safe, having sides. She had been crying. Her cheeks were smeared with tears and slush from her wet mittens. When Amelia picked her up, she was burning.

By nightfall the child had pneumonia, and three days later she was dead.

There was a certain amount of talk.

31

IT IS PAINFUL, waiting to see if you are chosen. In the last weeks before Track Week and the sorority invitations, Hilary felt that she deserved to feel better than she felt. She had worked hard that year and had done nothing wrong either in public or in private (knowing as she did that private wrongdoing does become public). She was certainly not going to be Valedictorian—Kathy was—but her grades were good and the Dean of Admissions had admitted her. Nothing could prevent her attendance at the University even if at the last moment she ran wild, which, in all honesty, she was not likely to do.

But being admitted was not enough. And in the meantime, she had lost some allies. After the child died, Amelia was not interested in much. Once you have graduated from high school you can do what you wish: sometimes Amelia said she would go back East and sometimes she said West. Sometimes she said she couldn't go anywhere because she could not leave Anne.

Kathy was ill-tempered. Her father's student was seen everywhere with someone more appropriate to his age. This more appropriate person had sleek black hair and worked in the Bon-Ton when she was not getting A's at the University.

Kathy said, "I don't give a darn about those parties. I won't be here anyway in the fall."

How come?

Kathy said, "It's your darned singing. Now he wants to go around and collect songs and then he will publish them and be an authority. And I," she added bitterly, "may never be educated. I may end up at U.C.L.A."

And Janet had defected. She was going to be a Chi Omega because a Chi Omega had made friendly gestures, and her mother had already sent to Salt Lake City for her evening gown.

Up until now, Hilary had received no friendly gestures.

May came, and the time was getting short. As in all other years, Mount Jumbo was topped with a pelt of green and a saddle of snow. On the Oval, dandelions broke out. The river rose.

One afternoon Hilary crossed over to see Doll. Everything felt odd and she would like to be with things familiar. Doll was ironing. Hilary helped herself to a saucer and sat down.

Doll said, "If you don't mind, don't put your ashes there. My father doesn't like it."

Hilary gave her a cold complaining look.

"Well, you know how he is," Doll said.

Yes. Hilary did know how he was. She said, "Are those new curtains?"

Doll turned and looked as if she hadn't noticed: perhaps trolls had brought them in the night. "Two years ago," she said. And shrewdly, for one who had never been very shrewd, "Perhaps you've just forgotten."

Hilary looked at her sharply, but she saw there was no malice in her words. Only acceptance. So it was probably all right for her to ask Doll something she wanted to know. Hilary, who still had hopes of Amelia, wanted to know what people were saying about Anne Lacey. How would Doll know? Well, Hilary suspected that Doll hung out in a lot of places she herself would not advise—beer parlors, hamburger joints. The Red Mill dance-hall. Places where people liked to talk about their betters.

But before she could ask, Doll put down the iron, hooked her soft hair behind her ear and said as if she were terrified, "I'm going to be married."

Who? But then Hilary saw it didn't matter a whit who. There was a time about fifth grade when they had vowed to be brides-maids for one another and had practiced getting married, had traipsed around in old lace curtains and hurled geraniums at one another. If one of them didn't catch the geraniums they tried again. They planned to have splendid dinner parties to which each would ask the other. The husbands too, of course.

Now there would be no dinner parties.

Of course Hilary still expected to marry when she got around to it and found somebody good. He would build her a house over around the Paxson School if that is where they were still building, though people were beginning to talk about Patty Canyon, and Patty Canyon was a pretty place. She had not thought much beyond that.

But her friend had.

Why, before Hilary had her degree, Doll might have children of her own, although that would depend on when she married. "When?" Hilary asked.

Doll said shyly, "Just as soon as we can afford."

Goodness, nobody can afford.

Then Doll's face flushed that pretty apricot and her eyes shone with an utter trust and a devotion such as Hilary had not seen— well, since she last had seen her parents. With all her heart she wished them well. Doll and whoever.

Then she went back across the street to tell her mother.

It did seem to Myra that once a woman gets them all out of the house and headed in their several directions and before she starts to clear, she should be able to finish her cold coffee and to read the paper. But the paper should offer pleasant things to read, such things as start a day off well.

She liked to read about weddings and about anyone who won prizes. Now, yesterday a little boy had won five dollars offered by the S.P.C.A., because his essay had been best. He wrote about a mother fox who could not come back to her litter because she was trapped. Myra was terribly sorry for the mother fox and also for the litter, but she was proud and happy for the little boy and obviously when he grew up he would be a kind man.

But today. The very first thing that had met her eye was that over around Idaho Falls a sheepherder had found an old Indian in an abandoned shack. Sometime before, the Indian had frozen to death. There is no reason for that. On the reservations the young ones are kind to the old, and the government, though heaven knows its hands are full, sees that they do not freeze. What touched Myra was to realize how much the old man had not wished to be on a reservation.

She turned the page.

A body had been found on the small island underneath the bridge. However did it get there? The people in the top floors of the Wilma Building never, never would throw their bodies there. It was suspected that it might have something to do with the cockfights over on that side of town. Some are poor losers.

She had just about decided to wrap the garbage in the newspaper, which would get rid of both. Hank wouldn't like it, because when he got home he liked his paper waiting. But if she blandly said that she had erred, who could gainsay her?

But then, tucked in between an ad for the Bon-Ton and one for the Emporium, she came across a thing so bad and unbelievable that she had no right to keep it from any of them.

FORMER MISSOULA HIGH SCHOOL TEACHER DEAD

Bizarre accident claims lives of . . . both. There was a cloudburst and a coulee and a Greyhound bus. Both Mr. Barry and his nice little wife. And others, too, whom no one in Missoula knew.

Myra's cup of cold coffee rattled in its saucer. She lowered it to the table carefully. Why, in a world where such can happen to friends and neighbors, who is safe?

All day she wandered about the house, answered the telephone, dreaded telling Hank, who was going to hate it so. As the day waned she went upstairs to freshen up and put a little toilet water on her wrists. Nothing is gained by acting differently. Then she glanced out the window and saw Hilary coming back from Doll's. It was surprising how her breath shortened. Just because you must be the bearer of bad tidings, that does not mean you yourself have done wrong.

On the landing Myra swayed a little and then leaned forward

to get her hand on the banister. She had some good news for Hilary, not just the bad news.

"Hilary," she called down. "A very well-spoken young woman called. About some little party? And Hilary, she left a number."

Below in the dim hall her daughter's bright hair smoldered.

"What number?" Hilary breathed.

"Oh goodness," Myra said, "I've got it right here somewhere."

She put her right hand in her apron pocket. Her left hand grasped the banister, except it didn't grasp but went on sliding. She crumpled easily, she fell as gently as it is possible for a large lady to fall down a flight of bare polished stairs. But she fell.

Nothing is supposed to happen to parents and any parent who allows a child to see something happen is remiss. Hilary had her strong young arms around her mother's shoulders.

"Don't move," she kept saying.

But of course Myra was going to move. As far as she could see, no harm was done. Everything that should wriggle, wriggled. However, a certain amount of harm was done because Hilary, who had not looked closely at her mother for some time, now looked closely and saw all the old bruises.

In a voice dreadful as her father's, Hilary said, "How long has this been going on?"

Myra said hardly any time at all and added that she would just as lief Hilary said nothing about it. But she saw that pretty soon they were all going to have to tell, because it wasn't fair. And one of them could come home to a nasty shock no thoughtful woman would want for them. However, it would have to wait.

Hank banged on the back door. It had to be Hank, it could not be Dan—Dan had been spoken to about banging. The moment she saw him standing there between the dining room and the living room, his face as pale as Hilary's under the rusted hair, she thought, *He knows.*

But then he said, "Where's the little boy?"

Why, it had not occurred to her! You see how selfish trouble makes you? But not dead, no. It is hard enough when grown people die. For a moment she saw the child tossed in the brown boiling waters of that coulee, arms and legs snapping like a doll's. No.

"Well," Hank said, "where is he? Why doesn't it say?"

"As to the first," Myra told him, "I'd guess with some authorities. Hank, no one in the world lets a child go uncared for."

He did not look convinced, unless of the unworldliness of his wife.

"As to the second, the way it's all squmped up makes me think they thought there wasn't any more room to say. But in that case, you'd think someone around the paper?"

It took a long time to get through, mostly because the girl at the switchboard didn't believe Hank. No, he didn't want circulation. No, he didn't want advertising. He wanted the editor.

"Mr. Ferguson?" she asked incredulously.

While he waited, Hank's hand whitened on the telephone. For a while in the background there were small busy noises and then something that sounded very much like a deep sigh.

"Just a minute," Hank said. He covered the mouthpiece with his hand and turned to his wife with such a stricken look that she knew. He did know about her.

He said, "We can afford help in the house. We can afford anything you want. We can afford the kid. Are you game?"

What he really wanted to know was, how long?

Long enough.

Myra nodded. She said, "We are all going to be game." For a moment his face was desolate as an abandoned homestead. Then the red pulsed in his cheekbones and he turned and shouted into the telephone.

"Ferguson," he said fiercely, "*I want that boy.*" Then Myra saw that Hank was going to be all right.

That is how Hilary began to learn that up until now she had learned nothing. That no one can afford self-pity, because that most expensive of commodities is always purchased at someone else's cost. And that there is no help at all against the random buffeting of chance.

When in good time she started her own letter like the letter her mother didn't know Hilary knew about, she knew how she would start.

Link arms and stand together. The rest is poppycock.

32

AMELIA KEPT SAYING, "If I had just been home." With her new wisdom Hilary said, "It wouldn't have made any difference. There would have been a next time."

Amelia said, "Really?"

She had taken to nibbling at the ends of her hair. Instead of falling in a black shiny sheath, it looked nibbled.

"Really," Hilary said.

Amelia had also taken to repeating things. "If I had just been home," she said. "It's my fault."

"It isn't anybody's fault," Hilary said. In a world where the innocent are vulnerable as the guilty, how can you speak of anybody's fault?

Hilary asked the boy who wished to go to Yale if he could explain this to her.

He said he couldn't.

Ah, but although Amelia's lovely mother kept telling her the same thing, her eyes meant otherwise.

"Darling, it wasn't anybody's fault." And she would take Amelia's hands in her white slim hands and look directly into Amelia's eyes with her smoky long-lashed eyes. "Always remember. It was nobody's fault."

Of course she did not know what Amelia had vowed to her father. "I will take care of them," she had said. Look at what happened. On the way to the hospital with the baby shaking in her arms she had crooned, "There, there. There. Everything's all right."

Well, it wasn't. Her little sister gasped and choked and died. Because Amelia had not been vigilant.

And now her mother grieved. But from her grief she drew more strength than Amelia had thought was there to draw. Anne kept busy. No longer withdrew into her room. Holding her glossy dark head high she went downtown and shopped the aisles of the Emporium and spoke to old friends. She bought bathing suits and Indian belts heavy with beads and summer dresses colored like sweet peas. And she began to speak about Amelia's graduation.

Amelia had no interest in graduation. It was hard to keep her mind on exams. She missed the child very much. The child had had a way, when Amelia studied, of nestling silently against her; she was trusting and smelled sweet. Amelia had loved her all along and hadn't noticed, and for that too, she was at fault.

"Oh no," her mother said. "You're going to pass and you are going to attend." If Amelia were not up there in her best before everyone, there were those who would say she had not passed.

Amelia would do anything for her mother. She was so proud of Anne and fearful for her, because Anne was steel by day but at night she still drove too far and too fast. Now that the languorous nights were here again, sometimes she did not get back till dawn. On those nights Amelia lay awake and listened. She wished that her mother would stay home and be comforted, but there is no comfort for one who has lost a child.

"I think this time," Anne said, "we'll go to Mrs. Prince."

The fact is that no one can be dressed in Missoula unless you go to Mrs. Prince. It was not always so. At one time you could go to Butte and some still thought that they could get away with Denver. But an unguided lady could make great errors even in New York, and while the Emporium provided all necessities, those who wished to be dressed sought out Mrs. Prince, who went to Paris and to Texas for them. Her small shop, in the heights of the Wilma Building, many had never seen. Many cannot afford.

Even among the few who could afford, almost nobody wanted to buy her daughter a dress from Mrs. Prince and then conceal it under a cap and gown.

The caps and gowns had to be rented and shipped all the way from Seattle, Washington: surely that was enough.

Because Amelia had grown so skinny, her dress had to be altered. While she looked down at the gleaming part in Mrs. Prince's goldened hair, her mother regarded gloves that were displayed under glass like jewels. Or with her slim fingers silently played the scales on the arm of the velvet love seat where she sat. Or rose and brooded down upon the roof of the Emporium across the way. Mrs. Prince employed those who would alter, but some customers she herself liked to fit.

"And just as well for this one," she said over her shoulder. "Dear, can't you stand still? And Mrs. Lacey, she'll need others."

Yes, of course. Amelia should have reminded her. Critically, she appraised her daughter, who belonged to her and should be properly displayed. Something would have to be done about her hair.

Lately Amelia had begun to shake. Feeling her mother's gaze, she straightened her shoulders and made tight fists, but the more rigidly she tried to stand the more the satin, like water, trembled about her knees.

Mrs. Prince rose, pink-faced.

"Nervous little thing, isn't she," she said. "For her age."

So Anne had to do something about Amelia before people started talking about her just as they had talked about the other one. Besides, she could no longer bear that stricken look in which she read suspicion. She had told Amelia and had told her that what had happened was nobody's fault, unless it was Will Lacey's, who had given Anne a faulted child. Of course if Amelia had been home it wouldn't have happened, but that didn't mean it was Anne's doing. An Act of God is an Act of God: if things had not been set up like tenpins, nothing would have happened.

Did her own daughter have the effrontery to demand proof positive?

Well, that could be arranged.

That morning she stood in the hall of the old Lacey mansion, her hand still on the receiver of the telephone. The cavernous hall contained an elephantine sofa, a vast rug (in the days of dancing, it took three people to roll up that rug) and a massive gateleg table. Above, from the first landing of the stairway, high, thin stained glass windows threw down an ambiguous light. The telephone sat on the gateleg, which was skirted fore and aft by the floor-length panels that had made it possible to seat twelve when the great parties overflowed. Here and there straight chairs dwindled into the shadows. Anne Lacey doubted very much that Mrs. Phelps shifted that heavy furniture more than once a year. She wouldn't if she were Mrs. Phelps.

The call had been for Amelia. When the sororities asked you to the dances, they also asked if there were a particular friend you would like to bring? Or would you prefer they arrange that you be brought?

Amelia had no friend. But if someone attractive was arranged, perhaps she would begin to act more like a girl, and less like an accuser. Especially if Anne arranged the evidence.

First, on the pad upon which one left messages, she left the message. Amelia: call the Delta Gamma House. She dated it, because in that house that is what they did. Then from the back of the pad she eased a page, making sure that no small scrap adhered to the gummed binding to give away that anything had been removed. On this she wrote:

> *Mrs. Phelps—please call the school*
> *and have Amelia sent home. I have*
> *one of my heads.*

Thoughtfully, she dated it on the day that the child fell ill. Then with one slim buffed nail she flicked that message down behind the table, where it would not be found until she wished it found. You see? Pure accident. Nobody's fault at all. She would have done better to leave well enough alone.

As it turned out, Amelia did not go to that dance nor to any other: while the Delta Gammas asked her and the Thetas asked her, the Kappas did not.

"Jealous cats!" Anne said.

And would not permit Amelia to do what Amelia had thought that she would have to do; if Will Lacey's daughter did not appear at the Kappa house she would not appear anywhere and would go away in the fall. And so all during Track Week Amelia got to lie upon her bed and listen to the horns and music from the Sigma Chis on the next block assault the summery air and the hateful dresses in the closet stirred like wraiths.

On the evening of graduation day she lay there once again. The purple gown was draped upon a chair, the purple cap with the gold tassel sat upon its lap. How was she to mount those shallow steps, cross, hold the rolled parchment in one hand and with the other shake the hand of Mr. Gilpin?

Mrs. Phelps entered her room without knocking. She had never done that before. Amelia was startled because she was not used to the fact of Mrs. Phelps in her room. Nor to a Mrs. Phelps with a flushed face and bobbing head. Everyone looks different where one does not expect to see them. The druggist looks odd on the bus; one does not recognize the dental assistant who is buying gloves where you are buying stockings. And you may not recognize people who are angry, at least Amelia didn't, because she had not known that she knew angry people. Hilary had once told her that, and had not meant it as a compliment. Mrs. Phelps said she quit.

Amelia had often seen Mrs. Phelps annoyed, but not to the point of quitting. At such times she made brownies and waylaid Amelia, who had to eat them. They were pretty good. Her complaint was usually how much a body expected of a body with the house so big and Spud not the help he ought to be. She always simmered down.

Then she would say, "Don't tell your mother. I wouldn't want her to think I was thinking."

But today she quit. Anne Lacey thought her dishonest and perhaps incompetent? There are some who will not endure it. Traps! Threads across drawers and hairs in checkbooks! Papers to prove you haven't cleaned where you should clean!

Amelia knew her mother wouldn't do anything like that. She didn't care enough about the house. So she said gently, "Let me see."

It was her mother's handwriting, all right. The deadly date made her heart rattle against her ribs. The only sense it made was that she had been right all along: she had failed.

She said, "But if it's been there all along . . ."

Mrs. Phelps said, "It wasn't there Wednesday week."

Mrs. Phelps said whatever anyone believed, when she cleaned she cleaned and did it regular. Except for the attic, which got done once a year. More would be silly.

What did it mean?

"What do you want of me?" Amelia asked.

Why, to bear witness.

When she left trembling with wrath, Amelia was still trying to understand. It wasn't a reasonable thing for Anne to have done. What was the purpose of it? What was it meant to reveal? Or to conceal?

There was a way to find out. She would ask.

Anne Lacey, clad for graduation, sat beside her telephone. She wore a pongee suit the color of a tanager. For a graduation, most mothers would wear something drabber, but then, most mothers were more drab. She put the receiver up suddenly.

She said, "You aren't dressed?"

Amelia said, "There's something I don't understand."

Anne said, "What do you mean?"

Amelia handed her the paper.

Anne's long lashes hid her eyes. Then she looked brightly at her daughter. She said, "Oh, thank God." That was not a phrase that she usually used. She said, "I knew I'd tried to get you home. I could have sworn. But you know my heads."

No. Amelia knew almost nothing about her mother. She stood there, a tall thin girl nervously rubbing her hands together. The early evening light struck through the thin lace curtains and picked out the shepherd simpering to the shepherdess. It lay like a gold shawl across the big four-poster bed and glinted on Anne's sleek black hair and on the small jeweled watch that she raised to her eyes. Upon the mantel the big hand of the gilded clock danced down its palsied way.

You cannot plan a death. But you can let it happen.

Her mother rose slowly, her slim ankles firm on her tilted heels. Her lovely face was cold. She said, "Are you accusing me of something?"

Until that moment, Amelia had not been sure.

Outside the windows and across the lawns the light suddenly yellowed, as it does on summer evenings. Inside, the old rug was arsenic and the pier glass lemon. In that glass Anne Lacey's scarlet dress stained the soiled reflection of the curtains.

Anne said, "Was it so wrong to think that you would watch your sister?" After a moment she said, "Well?"

Something disintegrated between them. A kindness, a gentleness, a loyalty that, come to think of it, never existed. Once that thought wormed its way into her mind, Amelia knew that it was true. Since her father died, she had been trying to buy peace. But from people like Anne you cannot buy peace because they don't have it to sell. As if she read her daughter's mind, the woman's face tightened.

She said, "Aren't you already responsible for enough?"

Her mother didn't like her.

Amelia said, "For what?"

Anne Lacey's fingers interlaced. She said, "I may damage myself."

"No, you won't," Amelia said. "You never do."

She didn't like her mother.

Cat's eyes. Anne said, "I don't have to take this from you."

Cat's spring. She slammed the door behind her and she locked Amelia in. What good was that supposed to do? All that Amelia had to do was to call the carriage-house.

But she couldn't, because Spud wasn't there. Spud was already off in his bib and tucker to see her graduate High. She heard the

Pierce Arrow snarl through the gate that was no longer locked. Anne wanted to frighten her. Why, she was dangerous as a child.

There are so many ways that one may damage oneself. Drink will do it, or sleeping pills or simple speed . . . *her father's gun was at the lake.*

One should not challenge children. They are the ones who say, "I'll show you."

Amelia went to the window and lifted out the screen. It was a tall house and a long way down. The clock spoke the quarter hour.

If you hung by your hands you could drop to the roof of the veranda and if you didn't roll, from there you could use the thin pillars of the porch; maybe the hop vine would help, although the frail new tentacles didn't look as if they had much purchase. If you rolled you would break something and lie there helpless.

That would be dandy. That would be just swell.

Myra had sprinkled talcum down her dress and had found Hank's good shoes and congratulated herself because she had not disposed of Dan's blue serge Sunday suits as he outgrew them. She had found one that fit the little boy. He looked frightened, but pretty soon he would not be frightened. She told him he looked fine and for a moment she held him to her soft side. Then she told Hank she wanted to leave a little early.

She said it might be hard to park. Hank said no, it wouldn't. He would drop them off and she could scoot right in and hold a place for him. Myra said if the auditorium filled fast they might find themselves behind one of those posts that held up the balcony. Hank said he would sit behind the post. He said he didn't want to be there forever.

Myra said forever wouldn't be long enough. "Hank, she's so beautiful tonight."

"Yes, she is," he said. "I'll bring the car around."

And so Amelia's call rang through the empty rooms without disturbing the dust motes that hung upon the lessening light.

Janet's mother said "Damn!" and her father pretended not to hear. They both felt he had earned the right to see his one child graduate, though he was a nice man and did hope the patient wasn't very ill. They drove right over and picked up Kathy's parents, who were waiting on their porch. Kathy's mother thought Janet's mother was dull as ditch water but had not refused the ride. Getting around town is one thing in oxfords and another thing in heels.

So then Amelia called Doll.

Four rings. Five. Then Doll's voice, breathless. "Gee, kid, I was out the door."

Then Doll said, "Con and me will be right there."

But first they had to explain to Con's Dad, who was wearing his good suit.

Con's Dad said to drop him off downtown. He said the important thing was the diploma and not necessarily to see the person getting it. He said that after they got to the old Lacey mansion and found Amelia gone.

All through the Hellgate her head was spinning and her driving bad. Cars blasted indignantly as she passed. Those cars were going too fast too, but then, everyone goes too fast. At Bonner she took the turn by the sawmill too sharply and the small car slipped and drifted but she got it back. After that she slowed and settled in to the long drive, because she had to get there.

Her mother would not attempt anything in the way of damage until Amelia was there to be sure that she failed. Oh, she was sure of that. But if Anne got bored waiting, she might hide. She might let Amelia wonder about the deep black lake. Hilary said you can stand anything you have to stand, but that was one thing that Amelia wasn't sure she could stand: if Anne hid from her. Like the child.

And then Amelia reproached herself. Her mother's life was harsh enough without her harshness. She had long turned the headlights on; the high cold air was spicy. She left the open land that was bare as the moon and tunneled through the tamaracks. Maybe Anne hadn't known that she would follow. Maybe she knew she was judged and rejected and perhaps she thought, deserted, but Amelia would not desert because the cold fact was that the strong may not desert. An unexpected thought bobbed like a bubble: now she will love me.

Her mother's car nudged the shoulder of the road. Quietly, so that she would not startle Anne into an accident—her slim hand might this moment rest on Will Lacey's gun—Amelia eased down the bank and to the square of light that lit the darkness like a little stage.

She had been wrong, all right.

What she saw was domestic disarray. Her mother had kicked off her pumps and removed her scarlet jacket. What she held in her hand was not the Smith & Wesson but a fan of playing cards. While Amelia watched she slapped a card triumphantly upon the table top, tossed back her head upon the slim throat that was stretched as for the knife, and laughed at the man.

Her anger drove Amelia back up the bank with an avalanche of chattering pebbles. If they heard, so much the better. She turned her car with a screech of tires even Anne Lacey could not have matched, and headed back toward town.

Oh, she would show them.

Doll felt pretty silly jouncing along in the truck in her long white dress and slippers. Myra had bought the slippers for her. "Nonsense," Myra said. "It's a graduation present." Con said he didn't give a tinker's dam but he did wonder even if they caught up, what they were supposed to do.

Doll said they wouldn't know until they caught up.

Con said he hoped that in the future she was not going to want to see a whole lot of people like Amelia. He peered ahead and kept his hand on the gearshift at all times. She felt that he was very harsh and dependable.

They passed the Indian reservation and the bison range and then, just before the turn through the tamaracks they saw Amelia's car, which was upside down in the barrow-pit. The wheels were still spinning, but slowly, and even before they scrambled from the truck, the wheels gentled and were still.

So one of us is dead: the rest are dandy.

A lot of things in Montana changed after that. For one thing, Anaconda Copper pulled out. During the wars the young surged out to the coast to work for Boeing, but when the last one ended they came spilling back. The big bright skies over the Missoula Valley are polluted now, and the encircling hills often cup a malodorous mist.

Strange. Not one of us lives in Missoula.

Hilary stayed with Myra as long as Myra lived. By that time everyone said it was a mercy, but Hank and Hilary never thought it was a mercy. Then she went back East and married the young man at Yale. She never did become a Kappa Kappa Gamma, but nobody seemed to mind at Yale.

Janet found someone perfectly plausible.

Kathy knows everything there is to know about the Restoration drama and has her doctorate. Hilary hears from her, now and again.

So that takes care of four of us but, if you remember, we were five.

Who do you think is the Queen of Grass Valley?

Readers' Guide for

The Girls from the Five Great Valleys

Discussion Questions

1. Who is narrating The Girls from the Five Great Valleys? What role does she serve in the novel?

2. Which of the five girls do you think the narrator liked best, and why?

3. What does the setting (both time and place) mean to the novel? Would the novel have been significantly different if it had taken place in, say, Detroit or Denver, or the place where you grew up?

4. How does the time period of the novel—the 1930s, deep in the Depression—affect the plot?

5. Who is the Queen of Grass Valley?

Suggestions for Further Reading

For me, one of the most enjoyable parts of *The Girls from the Five Great Valleys* is the friendship among and between the five girls. If you liked that aspect, too, try these:

In *The Cheerleader*, Ruth Doan MacDougall limns the ups and downs of high school loves and friendships in 1950s small-town New Hampshire.

Divine Secrets of the Ya-Ya Sisterhood by Rebecca Wells is the story of four friends—Vivi, Teensy, Necie, and Caro—growing up in Louisiana in the 1930s.

Probably the classic novel about women's lives and friendships is Mary McCarthy's *The Group*, which describes what happens to a group of eight young women in the first seven years after their graduation from Vassar College in 1933.

If what you enjoyed was the unique narrative voice, try these novels:

Reif Larsen's *The Selected Works of T. S. Spivet* is narrated in by T. S. himself, a twelve-year-old genius cartographer, who describes the events before and after he finds himself named the winner of a prestigious award from the Smithsonian (the judges didn't know how old he was).

The Virgin Suicides by Jeffrey Eugenides is told in a first person plural voice ("we"), as a group of boys in an upper-class suburb of Detroit in the 1970s reflects back from middle age on the defining moments of their adolescence: the fates of the five mysterious Lisbon sisters.

Also told from a first person plural voice is Joshua Ferris's very funny *And Then We Came to the End*, as cubicle-housed employees at a Boston ad agency face layoffs (due to the bursting of the dot-com bubble) in their ranks with anything but equanimity.

Eleanor Brown's *The Weird Sisters* uses two different voices to tell the story of the three Andreas sisters—Rosalind, Bianca, and Cordelia (their father is a Shakespeare scholar); the sisters combine to narrate the story of their lives together in a first person plural voice, while a third person omniscient narrator looks at each sister individually.

If what you enjoyed was the Montana setting, try these:

Ivan Doig's *This House of Sky* is a memoir of growing up in the part of Montana nearest to the Rocky Mountains of Colorado, at just about the same time period as Savage's characters in *The Girls from the Five Great Valleys* did.

Although I love the characters in Jamie Harrison's mystery *The Edge of the Crazies*, what I appreciated most was how she brought small-town Montana to vivid life. When a murder disturbs the placidity of Blue Deer, sheriff Jules Clement (archeologist turned lawman) tries to discover whodunit.

Life in the very small town of Shelby, Montana, over most of the first three-quarters of the last century is beautifully evoked in Deirdre McNamer's *One Sweet Quarrel*. (It's another of the Book Lust Rediscovery series.)

About the Author

Elizabeth Savage was the acclaimed author of such novels as *The Last Night at the Ritz*, *Summer of Pride*, *But Not for Love*, *A Fall of Angels*, and *Happy Ending*. Her writing has also appeared in *Redbook*, *Cosmopolitan*, *The Paris Review*, and several English and Canadian publications. She lived most of her life in Maine and married the novelist Thomas Savage. She died in 1989.

About Nancy Pearl

 Nancy Pearl is a librarian and lifelong reader. She regularly comments on books on National Public Radio's *Morning Edition.* Her books include 2003's *Book Lust: Recommended Reading for Every Mood, Moment and Reason*; 2005's *More Book Lust: 1,000 New Reading Recommendations for Every Mood, Moment and Reason*; *Book Crush: For Kids and Teens: Recommended Reading for Every Mood, Moment, and Interest,* published in 2007; and 2010's *Book Lust To Go: Recommended Reading for Travelers, Vagabonds, and Dreamers.* Among her many awards and honors are the 2011 Librarian of the Year Award from *Library Journal*; the 2011 Lifetime Achievement Award from the Pacific Northwest Booksellers Association; the 2010 Margaret E. Monroe Award from the Reference and Users Services Association of the American Library Association; and the 2004 Women's National Book Association Award, given to "a living American woman who ... has done meritorious work in the world of books beyond the duties or responsibilities of her profession or occupation."

About Book Lust Rediscoveries

Book Lust Rediscoveries is a series devoted to reprinting some of the best (and now out-of-print) novels originally published from 1960–2000. Each book is personally selected by Nancy Pearl and includes an introduction by her, as well as discussion questions for book groups and a list of recommended further reading.